THE STORM EAGLE

It was her sort-of-cousin Campbell
Roberts whose home was Castle Eyrie,
but it was going to be left to him and
Chiara jointly—so Campbell *decided*
that the solution to the problem was for
the two of them to marry. Without, of
course, consulting her! Which was a
pity, for in other circumstances Chiara
would not have been altogether unwilling. But now, of course, wild horses
wouldn't make her accept him.

THE STORM EAGLE

BY

LUCY GILLEN

MILLS & BOON LIMITED
15–16 BROOK'S MEWS
LONDON W1A 1DR

First published 1980
Australian copyright 1981
Philippine copyright 1981
This edition 1981

© Lucy Gillen 1980

ISBN 0 263 73613 x

Set in Linotype Times 10 on 11 pt.

Made and printed in Great Britain by
Richard Clay (The Chaucer Press) Ltd,
Bungay, Suffolk

CHAPTER ONE

CHIARA MANTI was determined not to be deterred from enjoying the magnificent Scottish scenery by her companion's apparent preoccupation with other matters. It was something of a surprise that it struck her as vaguely familiar after so long, and now that she was older she was more appreciative of its grandeur, something she was determined to enjoy despite Campbell Roberts' taciturn company.

Despite her name and her colouring Chiara was half Scottish, and this was by no means her first visit to her mother's native country, though it was the first time she had come alone. Seven years was a long time, and it seemed much longer because of all that had happened since her last visit.

A little over a year before, a tragic accident had robbed her of the three people she loved best in the world. Both her parents, in the company of her paternal grandfather, had set off one sunny April morning to attend a meeting at one of the minor motor-racing circuits, and she had never seen any of them alive again. Not sharing their enthusiasm for the sport, Chiara had chosen to stay home and so had escaped the carnage that resulted when one of the racing cars spun off the track and ploughed into the watching crowd before bursting into flames.

She had adored her parents and her Italian grandfather, and the first few weeks after the tragedy still remained a blank in her mind. Eventually she had brought herself to the realisation that for her at least life must go on, but her emotions still got the better of her sometimes and she tried not to think back too often.

5

Ian Roberts, her Scottish grandfather, had flown to Italy for his daughter's funeral despite his great age, and he had only reluctantly gone back to Scotland without her, so that Chiara hadn't the heart to turn down his latest invitation. It would do her good to get away for a while, and nowhere offered a greater contrast to her sunny native Tuscan hills than Castle Eyrie; also she was genuinely fond of the old man she had seen so seldom during her childhood.

Ian Roberts had been married twice. The first time was to his childhood sweetheart whose death when their only son was eleven years old had shattered him, so that to some his remarriage scarcely a year afterwards seemed incomprehensible. His second wife had been his secretary for many years and she not only knew him well, but loved him too, perhaps more than he had realised. It was from his second marriage that his only other child was born, a daughter called Marie, who eventually became Chiara's mother.

It was old Ian's grandson from his first marriage who was now driving her to Castle Eyrie and, as she had always done, Chiara regarded Campbell Roberts with wariness and not a little awe. The last time they met he had been twenty-five years old and impressive enough to completely overawe a petite twelve-year-old. She could still recall quite clearly hearing him demand of his grandfather just what he was expected to do to keep the black-eyed brat amused, and Chiara had never quite forgiven him that.

Whether or not it was Campbell himself who was giving her most cause for apprehension at the moment was debatable, however, for she felt almost as much in awe of his formidable mother. Margaret Roberts had no love for her father-in-law's second family, and did little to disguise the fact. In fact old Ian Roberts had doted on his lovely daughter and despaired her loss when Marie married her Italian tutor at university and went to live in her husband's country.

Margaret Roberts suspected all foreigners, and to her Chiara was one just as much as her father had been, even though she was old Ian's granddaughter. Part of her dislike arose from a fear that Ian Roberts might decide to divide his estate between his grandchildren instead of leaving it all to her son Campbell, as she felt he should do.

In ignorance of her reason, Chiara knew only that the big, rawboned woman whom she very reluctantly addressed as Aunt, disliked her and had never taken much trouble to hide the fact from her. Of course Chiara's looks didn't help to endear her to her aunt either, for she showed very little of the Roberts influence except for her clear light skin. Her hair was as black as her father's had been and her eyes too were so dark and lustrous they appeared almost black. Even her figure, slender though it was, showed a tendency towards soft Latin voluptuousness rather than the more angular leanness of the Roberts.

She was barely five feet two in height and a very pretty girl who would probably be a stunning beauty in a few years' time, just as her mother had been. It was because she was unaccustomed to being ignored quite so determinedly by the opposite sex that her companion's mood rankled so much. Not that she had any special desire to attract Campbell Roberts as a man, but it was not a situation she was used to, and the glance she gave him from the corner of her eye conveyed as much.

He must be about thirty-three years old, she realised, and he was what Chiara thought of as typically Scottish, although she wasn't quite sure what she based her opinion on. She made a swift and surreptitious study of him, and had to admit that he did have a certain earthy masculinity that was quite attractive; more attractive than she had realised.

He was very tall, about six feet two or three, she estimated, and his powerful physique slimmed down from broad shoulders to lean hips, with a broad chest fitted close under a grey-checked shirt. Obviously an outdoor man, he was tanned to the colour of teak, and in profile his face had a suggestion of harshness that contributed to her wariness of him, for the features were strong and craggy and there was a hint of temper in the wide firm line of his mouth.

His eyes, she recalled, were a bright vivid blue, like their grandfather's must once have been, but were at the moment half concealed by thick brown lashes. The set of his head with its red-gold hair suggested arrogance, and his jaw hinted at stubbornness. As a man he was impressive and rather alarming, and yet there was some indefinable something about him that attracted like a magnet, and seeing him for the first time from a more mature viewpoint, Chiara began to suspect that Campbell Roberts was far less unresponsive to her own sex than his present air of indifference implied.

Realising suddenly how closely she was concentrating on the man beside her, she made a resolute effort to turn her attention to the passing countryside instead. Soft green and blue hills had their heads wreathed in thin cloud that was just smeared across a summer blue sky, and the loch below the road they were travelling on looked deep and dark, reflecting the goat willow and gorse that covered the hillsides. It was beautiful country, but its softness was deceptive. Chiara knew from her mother; in winter it presented a much different picture, revealing a harshness below its gentle beauty.

'It's lovely countryside,' she ventured, and from the way Campbell jerked his head round to look at her, he might almost have forgotten she was there.

'You'll not remember it very much?' he said, then apparently decided there was no possibility of her doing so. 'No, of course you don't, you were only a school-girl and children forget such things.'

Colour warmed Chiara's cheeks and a sparkle of challenge showed in her dark eyes, for quite clearly he had made up his mind that she was still little more than a schoolgirl, and it was just one more thing about his whole attitude that rankled. 'It was seven years ago,' she reminded him, 'but as a matter of fact I remember some of it quite well. I was nearly thirteen, you know.' He passed no comment, and it was irresistible to voice something she had been convinced of ever since he had collected her from the airfield. 'You don't really like the idea of me coming to Castle Eyrie again, do you, Campbell?'

He arched one brow briefly and glanced at her from the corner of his eye. 'Now what makes you say that?' he queried, but Chiara noticed that he didn't deny it, and that seemed significant somehow.

Unable to give any specific reason for her suspicion, she shrugged. 'I can't say exactly,' she confessed, 'it's just—a feeling I have. Partly, I suppose, because you've scarcely spoken a word to me since I arrived.'

She noticed the corner of his mouth lift slightly as if he smiled, and something inside her recoiled from the idea of him finding her cause for amusement. 'I was simply going by the last time you were here,' he told her in the same attractively rolling accent that her own mother had retained to the day of her death, even after twenty years in a foreign country. 'I remember you always looked as if you expected me to gobble you up for breakfast. Or mebbe you did?' he suggested with a gleam in his blue eyes, 'and that's why you avoided me whenever you could.'

'You should be thankful I did!' Chiara retorted impulsively. 'It saved you the trouble of having to find some way of amusing the black-eyed brat!'

Obviously he had no recollection of the incident, which hardly surprised her, and he cocked a questioning brow at her. 'Am I supposed to know what that means?' he asked.

Chiara was already regretting her impulse, for Campbell Roberts wasn't the kind of man to challenge, and especially not on his home ground. In the circumstances Chiara kept her eyes on the scenery and tried to sound as casual as she was able. 'Oh, I overheard you asking Nonno Roberts one day what on earth you were expected to do to amuse the black-eyed brat.'

'And you've remembered that all this time?' He darted her a swift curious look and she had little doubt that he found it vaguely amusing. 'Well, it only goes to show that listeners hear no good of themselves, doesn't it?'

Chiara's dark eyes glowed with resentment and she pushed a fall of dark hair back from her forehead. 'I hadn't much choice,' she informed him. 'You weren't bothering to keep your voice down and Nonno's door was open; I couldn't help overhearing!'

He was evidently unperturbed and that ghost of a smile still lingered in his eyes when he looked at her again. 'Oh well, that's all water under the bridge now, and at least you've learned to say bo during the last seven years.' He caught her puzzled look and shook his head. 'You're obviously not as fluent as you sound,' he observed. 'It's an old saying—wouldn't say bo to a goose, meaning you lacked spirit.' Giving her no time to remark on his opinion, he pressed on, 'And I think it might be better in the circumstances if you called him Grandpa instead of—whatever the word is you use.'

'Nonno?' Chiara admitted the truth of the statement even though she resented his making it, but she wasn't going to yield automatically as he probably expected her to. 'Nonno Roberts has never objected to my using it,' she told him, 'so I don't see why you should.'

He gave her another swift sideways glance and Chiara noticed that his eyes were slightly narrowed, as if her defiance was unexpected. 'I see,' he said quietly. 'Well, you suit yourself, of course, but I can't promise that the old man won't tell you himself now that you're a wee bit bigger and not so much like a baby doll!'

'If he does, then I'll change to Grandpa,' Chiara told him.

A deep, quiet breath of laughter startled her into turning her head swiftly, and her cheeks coloured warmly as she sought for the cause of it. 'So you're still a wee bit afraid of him after all,' he commented. 'I thought you couldn't have become that much more brave than you were seven years ago!'

'I was *never* afraid of him!' Chiara denied indignantly. 'I had no cause to be afraid of *him*!'

'Of me?' He sounded far too much as if the idea pleased him, and Chiara's childhood wariness of him reasserted itself as she gave him a hasty glance from the corner of her eye. 'Were you really frightened of me, Chiara?'

Chiara's heart fluttered a warning, and she wondered if she was imagining the suggestion of cruelty she attributed to him or if it really existed. She was far more self-confident than she had been seven years before, but he was very much an unknown quantity and it dismayed her to realise that her grown-up self found him disturbing in a way she preferred not to admit to.

'I wouldn't say I was exactly afraid of you,' she denied, 'but it was all very strange to me here, and I was very young.'

His head turned again, but this time it was for no casual survey. Instead his vivid blue eyes travelled slowly over her from the crown of her black head to the creamy vee at the neck of her dress, and the sheer blatant arrogance of it sent little shivers along her spine. 'You still look very young,' he said. 'How old are you, Chiara?'

Chiara's tongue flicked across her lips in sudden agitation. 'I'm twenty—just. My birthday was a couple of weeks ago, and I'm old enough to resent being——' She broke off because she suddenly suspected he might find any kind of objection to his scrutiny amusing. 'Anyway, I'm not twelve any longer, so you don't have to worry about keeping the black-eyed brat amused on this occasion!'

When he glanced at her this time thick lashes concealed whatever was in his eyes, but a faint smile still touched his lips. 'We'll see,' he murmured. 'It could be a lot more fun this time!'

Chiara kept her gaze firmly on the passing scene, trying to do something about the way her heart was clamouring, for no man she had ever met had aroused so many complex reactions in her as he did. It wasn't easy crossing swords with him, and yet oddly enough it made her feel more alive than at any time since her parents died, and that didn't make much sense, she felt.

A sudden sharp turn in the steep road made her grab for the door and in her alarm suspicion reared its ugly head. Another and even sharper bend made her grab the handle and she darted a swift look at her companion, her heart thudding wildly. To her it seemed that the car was about to go off the road, but strong hands brought it swiftly and easily under control again.

'You shouldn't hold on to that handle,' he told her quietly and without looking round at her. 'It opens the door and you could be thrown out.'

Before he finished speaking he drove the car to the very edge of the road and braked it smoothly to a halt, while Chiara looked at the craggy profile he presented with wary eyes, that flutter of suspicion still curling in her stomach. Of course he hadn't meant her to be thrown out, it was nonsense to even think it, but there was something quite ruthless about the big man beside her that still overawed her and made her wary of him.

He turned in his seat and regarded her steadily for a moment, then leaned across her, his body forcing her back against the seat; hard, warm and unexpectedly affecting. 'What—what are you doing?' she faltered.

She raised her eyes to the arrogant brown face only inches from her own and her lips were parted, her breathing uneven. 'Better safe than sorry,' he murmured. 'It would be a pity to lose you so soon, wouldn't it, eh?'

The deep softness of his voice with its rolling accent, and the hard pressure of his body, were a potent combination and did strange things to her senses, yet the sensation uppermost at the moment was a kind of fear. She knew what he appeared to be doing, but suspicion had become firmly implanted and she again passed her tongue over dry lips, for in her mind's eye Campbell Roberts was as primitive and ruthless as any of his barbaric ancestors.

'I'm fastening the door to make sure I don't lose you,' he assured her in a deceptively soft voice, and his breath warmed her mouth, he was so close. 'What did you think I was doing, Chiara?'

She shook her head dumbly, unable to find words, and after a moment or two he slid back behind the wheel and started up the engine again. Shaken and without being quite sure why, Chiara clasped her hands together tightly and tried to concentrate on the countryside instead of Campbell Roberts.

They drove on down a steep hill and just below them at the lochside snuggled a tiny hamlet that she felt sure she remembered. Roberts' Brae, she recalled; almost everything around here was named for the Roberts, who had once owned as far as the eye could see. They hadn't much further to go now, and when she raised her eyes she caught her first glimpse of Castle Eyrie, perched like the eagle's nest it was named for, at the far end of the loch. Mellow and ancient, its old walls were partly hidden by trees and the ivy that had been allowed to cover its walls.

The road they were following continued on around the loch, but always in sight was that soaring hill at the far end. Its lower slopes were covered in dark swathes of Scotch pine, a narrow break defining the approach to the secluded grandeur of Castle Eyrie which the Roberts had held for the last three hundred years. In the days before the ubiquitous pine had become established, the castle had stood like an eyrie on the green hillside, commanding a view over the whole surrounding countryside. And no matter what other doubts plagued her, Chiara felt a certain pride when she saw it because she felt a part of its history.

'Castle Eyrie,' she breathed, and Campbell turned his head and looked at her.

'It impresses you, does it?' he asked and, not quite following his meaning, Chiara looked at him curiously.

'It's very impressive,' she said. 'But I was remembering that my mother was born there.'

'So was I, and I still live there!'

Chiara was sure he was trying to tell her something, but for the moment she couldn't imagine what it was, and she was distracted suddenly by a notice at the roadside. CASTLE EYRIE, she read as best she could for the crowding branches of the trees, SCOTTISH WILDLIFE RESERVE. VISITORS WELCOME. There was something else too in smaller print, but she had no time to read any more.

'A game park!' Chiara frowned at him curiously as he turned at the end of the loch and left the public highway for a narrow and much rougher route that ran right up through the woods to the castle. Not all the trees were pine, she noticed on closer scrutiny, there were brakes of broad-leaved wood as well. 'This is new, isn't it, Campbell?'

'New since five years,' Campbell informed her. He had reduced speed to little more than five miles an hour and the car was labouring on the steep incline. 'You'd be surprised how many people are interested in seeing what Scotland used to be like.'

'I'd no idea anything like this had happened.' She glanced at his darkly tanned face, shadowed still more by the close crowding trees, and speculated. 'Your idea?' she guessed.

Her grandfather was still titular head of the family, and presumably the estate would go to Colin, his son, when he died, and yet Campbell had the air of a man who was very much involved, and she felt certain the reserve was his idea. He was not the kind of man to take kindly to serving someone else, she felt, and consequently wondered just what the situation was at Castle Eyrie now.

Something moved among the trees, and Campbell slowed the car almost to a standstill while he pinpointed a small round-headed creature with a long body and bright inquisitive eyes. But even before Chiara had time to see it properly it went scampering along a branch and whisked out of sight leaving an impression of pale fur on throat and breast.

'A pine marten,' said Campbell, increasing speed slightly. 'They breed here, and that's quite an achievement.' He gave her a brief glance over his shoulder. 'And yes, it was my idea—do you mind?'

'Mind?' She couldn't imagine why he asked that, and looked at him curiously.

'Well, you will eventually own half of it,' Campbell told her with a touch of impatience. 'Good grief, girl, don't you realise that's why you're here?'

Chiara hadn't had the slightest idea, and she used her hands in a very Italian gesture of denial. 'I—I don't know—I mean, I didn't even think about it. When Nonno – Grandpa asked me to come over I just thought he realised I needed a break from routine, and I haven't seen Castle Eyrie for a long time——'

A grim kind of smile touched his mouth for a moment and she thought she detected a hint of sadness in those uncannily blue eyes for a second before he spoke. 'Grandpa is eighty years old,' he reminded her, 'and he wants to put his house in order. My father——' He heaved his great shoulders hopelessly. 'Oh, Grandpa will explain it all when he's ready, but what it boils down to is that eventually you and I will share Castle Eyrie, and all it entails, between us.'

'I'd no idea.'

She felt a quite inexplicable flutter of anxiety suddenly, and something gleamed in the eyes that glanced at her for a moment that did not exactly help matters. Speculation perhaps, but also a hint of malice, she would have sworn. 'You *are* still very young, aren't you?' he commented. 'Well, that's the way it is—or will be, whatever anyone thinks about it.'

Chiara thought she understood suddenly. That rather dry observation gave her the clue she needed, and she could guess who took the worst possible view of a virtual stranger coming in to claim a half-share of what Margaret Roberts would almost certainly see as solely her son's inheritance. It was difficult to judge what Campbell's own reaction was to the idea, but certainly the thought of Aunt Margaret's opinion did nothing to improve the prospect of her visit, and she wished there was time to have second thoughts.

But with the castle already looming ahead of them it was too late, and there was something so mellow and inviting about the old place, grim as it had once been. It was not a castle in the usual sense of the word, although it did have two rounded turrets, one either side of its front elevation, and the door that faced them when they got out of the car was almost five inches thick and studded with iron bolts.

Tall narrow windows gave an impression of secretiveness, and the garden surrounding it was mostly of shrubs and red gravel paths, with only one or two flower beds to brighten the general air of sombreness. No one stirred, and in her imagination Chiara saw generations of Roberts striding up to that massive door and demanding instant obedience from those who served them. As she walked across the gravel with him she felt that Campbell Roberts fitted into the setting perfectly, much more so than she did herself.

She looked and felt very small beside his towering height, and strangely alien in her bright Italian silk dress and pretty coloured shoes. Somehow she had to find the courage to face Aunt Margaret again, and she wished she had someone with her who was more likely to understand and sympathise with the way she felt. Just for a moment as they mounted the worn stone steps together, she caught his eyes and found his expression unexpectedly knowing, as if he was waiting for her to pass some remark.

Instead she simply waited for him to open the huge door and allow her to pass into the wide shady hall. The last thing she expected was to feel his hand slide under her arm and the strong hard fingers curl lightly into her flesh, and she could do nothing about the wild erratic beat of her heart as they crossed the hall. High and wide, with plain white walls and carpeted underfoot, it was an impressive introduction to the building as a whole, and it too struck a note of familiarity.

A man emerged from the shadowy nether regions and

gave her a sideways glance from bright brown eyes, but he lingered only long enough for Campbell to give him instructions about taking her cases upstairs. They continued on into what Chiara privately remembered as the *salone*, a room her mother had called the sitting-room.

Campbell's hand was still under her arm and she found it oddly reassuring, so that the thought crossed her mind that he might be aware of his mother's effect on her. It was a big room and an attractive one. The long windows were open to the garden and long streamers of sunlight picked out thinner patches in the carpet, but gave added richness to the beautiful old Jacobean furniture.

Colin Roberts was on his feet in a moment, coming across the room to her with his hands outstretched and a smile of welcome on his face. Here at least was a genuine welcome, Chiara felt, and it did wonders for her flagging spirits. Her uncle's features were so like her mother's had been that for a moment it brought a lump to her throat just seeing him—the same light grey eyes and red-gold hair, although Colin's was already streaked with grey, and the same warm smile.

'Chiara!' He held her hands for a moment then pulled her into his arms and kissed her warmly. He was a big man, like his father and his son, and Chiara remembered his bear-like hugs from her childhood. 'Och, you've grown prettier than ever,' he insisted. 'Hasn't she, Margaret?' He didn't wait for his wife's opinion, however, but while he went on talking, Chiara could feel the older woman's sharp eyes on her, critical as they had always been. 'Did you have a good journey, my dear? Personally I hate flying, but it does shorten the time between here and there, doesn't it? And mebbe one doesn't get quite so tired.'

While he talked they moved across to where Margaret Roberts sat, working at some kind of sewing which she apparently put aside only grudgingly while she shook hands. There would be no hug and kiss from her aunt, only the formality of a handshake, and Chiara could remember how the greeting had chilled her as a small child accustomed to warmth and affection.

'How are you, Chiara?'

'Very well, thank you, Aunt Margaret.'

She did not like being addressed as Aunt Margaret, Chiara recalled, but nothing was said against it at the moment, and her uncle was intent on chattering if no one else was. 'You remind me so much of your mother, my dear,' he said softly, and squeezed her hands. 'It was such a tragedy she died so young, and your father too, he was no age to die.'

He had been fifteen years older than her mother, Chiara recalled, but they had been an idyllic couple through all the more than twenty years of their marriage, and she doubted if her uncle had known as much happiness with his hard-faced Margaret. 'I—I don't feel quite so badly now, Uncle Colin, but at first——' She took a firm grip on her trembling voice and shook her head. 'I was glad to be able to come and see you all again.'

'I imagine you know *why* you were invited?' Margaret Roberts' hard flat voice broke across her words, and her husband frowned.

'Not now, my dear,' he told her. 'There'll be plenty of time to go into that when Father joins us. For now I imagine Chiara would like to freshen up after her journey, wouldn't you, Chiara?'

'I would rather, I feel a bit travel-stained.'

'In fact you look quite fresh and very lovely,' her uncle assured her with a smile. 'You've left half the young men in Tuscany pining for you, I've no doubt!'

He made her feel so much more at ease than either his wife or his son did, and Chiara was grateful to him for that. 'I don't know about pining for me,' she smiled, 'but I think I might be missed, for a while at least.'

'I'm quite sure of it, my dear!'

'You don't look like a Roberts.' Hostile grey eyes regarded her with undisguised dislike, and Chiara wondered how a man as nice as her uncle had come to marry such a woman. 'You're too much like your father.'

Chiara held tightly to her temper, an explosive Latin temper that was not always easy to control, and she was tempted to turn and leave there and then rather than stay with such an unwilling hostess. But her mother had been just as much old Ian Roberts' child as Colin was, and now that she knew what her grandfather had in store for her, she did not feel inclined to let this grasping woman drive her away from it.

'My father was a very handsome man,' she said in a voice she controlled only with difficulty. 'Thank you, Aunt Margaret.'

Unbelievably, she could have sworn that the look she saw in Campbell's eyes approved of her stand, and yet it was hard to understand in view of his earlier attitude. It was again unexpected when he slid his hand under her arm, pressing his long fingers into her flesh for a moment before he spoke.

'You'll mebbe feel better when you've freshened up,' he suggested. 'If you'd like to come with me, I'll show you where your room is.'

A murmured apology excused her, and she noticed that there was a smile almost of satisfaction on her uncle's face, a smile that changed swiftly to a frown when Margaret Roberts again left her feelings in no doubt. 'Essie can surely show Chiara her room, Campbell,' she said. 'You're not required to run around like a chambermaid!'

'Margaret!' Her uncle's voice crackled with anger, and knowing him only as a mild and gentle man Chiara blinked in momentary surprise. 'I don't think Cam would have offered if he didn't want to go,' he went on, his tone already quieter and more calm. Then he turned and smiled at them again, side by side in the doorway with Campbell appearing to bend protectively over Chiara's much smaller figure as he leaned down to the door-knob. 'You away and see your room now, Chiara,' Colin told her. 'We'll see you later.'

The silence they left behind them was ominous, yet Chiara suspected that she was much more aware of it than Campbell was as he strode across the hall with her. Neither of them said anything, but just for a moment when she glanced at him from the corner of her eye she found him watching her, and the small enigmatic smile she noted did little to make her feel more at ease.

The staircase was one of the things that Chiara remembered quite well from her earlier visits, for it was remarkably narrow and dark for the size of the place. Also its balustrades were made in solid oak panels that were darkened with age and bore relief patterns of leaves, thistles and jaunty cockades, an emblem deliberately used to cock a snook at the English during the Jacobite risings, and which intrigued her anew when she noticed it.

'Nervous?'

The solitary word was breathed warmly quite close to her left ear and it was instinctive to jerk aside from the intimacy it suggested. Meeting his eyes for a moment, she felt herself colour, and told herself that she was slightly breathless only because she was having difficulty keeping pace with him as they mounted the worn treads.

'A little,' she confessed cautiously. 'I haven't been here for seven years, and I don't have to be a clairvoyant to realise I'm not exactly welcome—at least by you and Aunt Margaret!'

'Me?' Chiara wondered why he bothered to question it, but his smile was faintly sardonic and he was regarding her again from the corner of his eye. 'You jump to an awful lot of conclusions, don't you!'

'You surely don't deny it?' she challenged, but was destined never to know whether or not he would have done.

They had reached the top of the stairs and as they stepped on to the long tiled passageway someone was leaving one of the many rooms that lined it. With a catch in her throat Chiara recognised her grandfather, but not the same man she had seen in Italy only a little over a year ago, for this man looked a good ten years older than he had then and he used a stick to help him walk.

'Nonno!'

The familiar Italian came automatically, and she left Campbell to go hurrying towards the old man who now stood peering along the ill-lit passage at them. Then he held out his arms, his face breaking into a smile, and she went running along to him to be clasped close for a moment and hugged in a silent embrace.

'Och, my poor wee girl!' He held her at arm's length and the need for a walking aid seemed to have been forgotten for the moment as he stood tall and only slightly bent, regarding her with faded blue eyes that had once been as vivid and bright as his grandson's. 'You look pale, child; you need some Highland air in your lungs and a brisk wind to bring colour to your cheeks.' He shook his head slowly, ignoring Campbell for the moment. 'Oh, but you're a pretty one,' the old man said softly. 'You're a real beauty, my bairn, aren't you?'

He hadn't looked close on eighty years old the last time she had seen him, but now he did, and Chiara hated the difference, however inevitable it was. He seemed to have shrunk somehow and his big frame lacked the flesh it needed to make him impressive, but the will was still there and showed in his eyes as he took her arm and steered her back towards the room he had just left.

'I've my own little sitting-room up here,' he told her as he opened the door, and just for a moment a wicked gleam showed in his eyes that likened him to his grandson. 'It keeps me out of folks' way and it gives me a bit of peace when I need it.' He turned and looked at Campbell over his shoulder. 'Are you coming to join us, Cam, or have you to get back?'

Just briefly Campbell switched his gaze to her, then he nodded his head, that suggestion of a smile in evidence again. 'I'll join you for a few minutes,' he agreed, 'if Chiara doesn't mind.'

'Why should she mind?' the old man demanded, but Campbell only smiled and shook his head again.

Ian Roberts took a chair only when he had seen Chiara seated, and Campbell hovered somewhere in the background, half hidden in the shadows formed by the contrast of bright sunlight from the windows, a big and slightly disturbing attendant that Chiara could not quite ignore. 'It's good to see you again,' she ventured. 'How are you, Nonno?'

There was no real need to ask, but she could do no other. He was old and no longer able to stride about as he had, or ride the horses he loved. Chiara herself had never learned to ride, but she had spent hours riding about the estate perched in front of her grandfather when she was a little girl, and she knew how much he must miss that sense of freedom.

The faded eyes smiled at her warmly, but they were touched with regret too, just as Campbell's had been earlier, and for the first time she began to realise just how similar the two men were. As a child she had found no similarity at all, and had felt affection for the older man, suspicion of the younger.

'I'm old, child.' The statement was chilling in its frankness and she felt a shiver trickle along her spine. 'There are things to be done before I'm much older, and I'd like you here for a while if you can spare me some of your time.'

Chiara had been born and raised in a warmer clime that encouraged more frank emotions, and she did not even try to conceal the tears that trembled just behind her lashes. 'Of course I'll stay!' she assured him impulsively. 'I'll stay as long as you want me to, Nonno!' She fluttered her hands vaguely when the looming presence in the shadow shifted slightly, and shook her head. 'I'm sorry,' she apologised huskily. 'I should call you Grandpa like Campbell does.'

The old man reached out and stroked a hand lightly down her cheek, and it was obvious he had not even heard her apology. 'You still look very Italian,' he murmured, half to himself, she suspected, 'but you have your mother's fine features and her complexion.'

He had loved his daughter dotingly, it was no secret, and it was one of the reasons why Margaret Roberts disliked his second family so much. Had his precious Marie not been born and in turn produced a daughter, there would have been no question of Campbell having to share Castle Eyrie and all it entailed. Mentioning her mother inevitably brought her to mind, and Chiara clasped the old man's hand tightly for a moment.

'She still missed Castle Eyrie, Grandpa, and she spoke of it often, and of you.'

In the past Ian Roberts had never been a sentimentalist, and he was not long pulling himself back from the brink of being maudlin. She saw him consciously pull back his slightly stooping shoulders and the familiar gleam was in his eye again as he looked at her. 'Aye, well, I'll not so readily see you go off back to Italy,' he told her. 'Now that you're here, you'll stay for good, I think.'

A little startled by his certainty and conscious of Campbell in the background, Chiara hesitated. There was something about the feel of the present situation that she did not quite understand and it made her uneasy. 'I—I don't know about staying permanently,' she demured, but the old man would brook no opposition.

'It isn't worth you paying the fare back,' he told her with fine Scottish thrift, and a finality that made her shiver. 'It'll not be very long now and the place will belong to you and Campbell. I've been called an autocrat, but I'm not conceited enough to suppose I'm going to live for ever!'

She could see now why Campbell had seen fit to forewarn her as far as he dared, and in a way she was grateful to him, for she would have been completely thrown had it been suddenly thrust upon her. As it was she found it hard to think clearly, or to follow his reasoning where the disposal of the estate was concerned.

'But surely——' She glanced across at Campbell's dark and barely discernible features and hesitated. 'Surely Uncle Colin is next in line? I mean——'

'Colin's just taken over the Campbell distillery,' her grandfather told her. 'At least, he's come into four-fifths of it, and that's not to be sneezed at. And you've no need to disturb yourself about it, for Colin's never had the interest in this place that young Campbell has, he's far more interested in the distillery, even though Margaret has a fifth share and never lets him forget it!'

Again Chiara had to adjust her ideas hastily. 'Aunt Margaret only has a fifth?' she asked, and automatically glanced at Campbell when she said it. 'But surely—her father's business——'

In fact it was Campbell who answered her and it was difficult to define the expression in his eyes because he still stood back in the shadows. 'Grandfather Campbell never forgave Mother for being a girl,' he told her, 'and it was even less in her favour that she was an only child. He'd rather see the family business come to the Roberts than let her have it—the mean-hearted old devil!'

It seemed hard to understand anyone sympathising with a woman like Margaret Roberts, but her son obviously knew her better than Chiara possibly could, and she allowed he was right to sympathise with her in the matter of her father's will. Her grandfather's sympathy, however, was unexpected and more revealing than he probably realised.

'Poor Margaret,' said the old man, shaking his head. 'Old John practically forced her to marry Colin for the sake of tying himself to the laird's family, and he'd not even the decency to make amends in his will. As Cam says, a mean-hearted old devil to the very end!'

It was a new and intriguing slant on the character of Aunt Margaret, and one that could only arouse Chiara's sympathy, for she was nothing if not soft-hearted. 'I didn't know anything of that,' she murmured, and her feelings were so obvious that her grandfather reached out and pressed a hand over hers.

'There's no need to feel too sorry for her,' he told her firmly. 'And if you're to stay here for any length of time you'd best not be unaware of what Margaret feels about you sharing Castle Eyrie with Campbell. She doesn't like it and she'll not hesitate to let you know it, I don't doubt, so don't let your soft heart run away with you, girl—hold your own or your life'll be made a misery for you!'

Her heart was beating hard and fast and Chiara wished she had known even half of what she now knew before she left her home in Italy. It was a new experience to be involved in the kind of feuding her mother's family evidently took in their stride, and she wasn't sure she could cope.

'Mebbe you'd rather go back to Italy?' Campbell's voice suggested softly from the shadows, and she jerked her head round swiftly.

Realising what was in his mind, she resented it and it

aroused a reaction in her that she did not at first recognise. Anger, resentment, a kind of pride, she supposed, and it was a moment or two before she recognised the same stubbornness in herself that characterised the two men with her. She was as much a Roberts as Campbell was, and if he thought he was going to chase her back to Italy while he laid claim to what was hers, he could think again.

'I'll be quite happy living in Scotland,' she assured him, and quite distinctly heard her grandfather's sigh of satisfaction.

CHAPTER TWO

BREAKFAST at Castle Eyrie was very different from the light rolls and coffee that Chiara was accustomed to, but so far she had managed to cope with the huge meals put before her without complaint. Had it not been for the reaction she suspected would arise from her request, she would have asked for something more in line with what she was used to, but she had no wish to cause a controversy so early in her stay.

It was completely unexpected when Campbell asked if she would like to accompany him one morning, and Chiara hesitated only because she wasn't sure what it might involve. She was in favour of conservation as far as it went, but she knew little about it, or about wild life in general.

'I thought you might like to see some of the changes we've made during the past five years,' said Campbell, as they all sat around the table after breakfast. 'Surely you're interested to see what we've done, aren't you, Chiara?'

'What *you've* done,' his mother asserted before Chiara could say anything. The past few days had done nothing to make her more kindly disposed towards her, and Chiara couldn't help regretting it, for her uncle's sake as much as her own. 'Everything that's been done is your doing and yours alone,' Margaret went on. 'You've worked like a slave to make it what it is, Campbell, though it's not been appreciated, that's obvious!'

The allusion was pointed and unmistakable, and she obviously felt very strongly about it, but while Chiara could understand her feelings to some extent, it was

28

none the less dismaying to be faced with such determined antagonism. She was less sure about Campbell's feelings, but there was a deceptive laziness about his smile when he answered.

'That's exaggerating a wee bit,' he said quietly. 'And it was Grandpa who put up the money for the initial outlay, remember. He worked too, for as long as he was able to—no, Mother, it wasn't all my doing by any means, although I suppose you could say I was the driving force behind it.'

He would be, Chiara thought. He sat across the table from her with his back to the window, and she cast him a fleeting glance as she rested her chin on one hand. A white shirt exposed the length of his brown throat and fitted closely across his broad chest, making her very aware of the body it covered, and there was something so disturbingly sensual about him that she almost shivered.

Big powerful hands supported his chin and his red-gold hair gleamed in the morning sunlight from the window. The small shadows that flitted across his features with every movement gave him a curiously preda-tory look that was incredibly affecting, and in the same vein his appraisal of her was distinctly and frankly earthy. He was a giant of a man and one she found herself drawn to almost in spite of herself.

'Mebbe you're not very interested in what we've done?' he suggested, and Chiara hastily snatched herself back to realities.

'Oh, but of course I am!'

'Then do you *want* to come with me?'

'Yes, of course, I'd love to,' she assured him. 'If as Nonno says I'm to have a half-share of it, I'd better start taking an interest.'

It was a rash thing to have said in Aunt Margaret's hearing, Chiara realised, for her aunt obviously saw the remark as a deliberate jibe, and she was immediately up in arms on her son's behalf, whether or not he needed her support. 'You have the—the nerve to taunt Campbell with it?' she demanded. 'He's to lose half of what should rightfully be his, and you have the nerve to sit there and taunt him with it? What kind of a woman are you, for God's sake?'

Chiara's hands clenched themselves tightly as she sought to control her reaction. She would never willingly have sought this kind of confrontation, and she did not normally take such a deep dislike to anyone, but despite all she knew about Margaret Roberts' situation, and the sympathy she felt for her, she simply couldn't condone her determined malice.

But the last thing she wanted was an outright quarrel, and she would have made a conciliatory move to end the situation, but Campbell was already taking a hand. 'Let it be, Mother, *please!*' He spoke very quietly and the hand he placed on his mother's arm was light and gentle, but it was clear that if it came to a battle of wills even her indomitable character would yield to her son's.

Nevertheless she left the matter reluctantly and the gleam of malice still showed in her eyes. 'I suppose you'll be down there all morning?'

'As usual,' Campbell agreed. 'When Chiara's had enough she can find her own way back.'

It was the kind of cavalier treatment she would need to get accustomed to, Chiara guessed as she got up from the table, and it was a natural progression to glance along the table to her uncle who was so much more gentle and kindly. 'I wish you were coming too, Uncle Colin. Don't you ever go and see what's going on down there?'

'Only very occasionally, my dear, but I've really no time for much else but the distillery these days.' Her grandfather, she recalled, had said that Colin was much more interested in the Campbell family business than in Castle Eyrie, and it seemed he was right. Colin clacked his tongue impatiently as he got up from the table. 'And it's high time I was away!'

'If you're ready, Chiara,' Campbell told her, 'we'll get going too. It'll mean more walking this morning if I've to take the Land Rover—I suppose you've not learned to ride a horse during the past seven years, have you?' Her brief shake of the head was greeted with a deep and, she suspected, very exaggerated sigh of resignation. 'Oh well, we'll just have to hoof it, then; come away, if you're coming, and don't let's be too late starting or Murdoch'll think I'm not coming!' His eyes scanned her slim shape in a beige skirt and yellow blouse and one raised brow questioned her. 'Do you need to make any changes before we go?'

Still not quite sure what to expect of the expedition, Chiara threw the onus back onto him. 'What do you think?'

'What I think is beside the point,' Campbell replied with a faint smile. 'As long as you can walk in those shoes, I'm not complaining about the rest of the outfit. Now will you come on, girl, before I give up and go alone?'

It was really too much, Chiara thought. He issued an invitation and then behaved as if she had asked to go with him, and she was about to point that out when she remembered that she hadn't seen anything of her grandfather yet. 'Should I go and say good morning to Nonno first?' she asked, and Margaret Roberts' voice cut in quickly ahead of her son.

'What did you call him?' she demanded, and Chiara turned, aware that Campbell was already standing in the doorway and frowning impatiently at the delay.

'*Nonno*,' she explained. 'It's the Italian word for grandfather, Aunt Margaret.'

Her aunt's eyes gleamed resentment. 'You speak

English,' she said, 'surely it isn't necessary to call your
grandfather by a foreign name.'

Chiara clung grimly to her rising temper, for she knew
she would be sorry if she spoke without stopping to
think. 'It isn't a foreign name to me, Aunt Margaret,'
she told her quietly, 'it's one I'm accustomed to using.'

'Margaret, my dear,' Colin Roberts broke in smoothly,
'must we make quite such a point of the fact that Chiara
is Italian by birth and upbringing? I'm sure Father
doesn't mind—whatever it is, so why should we?' He
gave another hasty glance at his watch and sighed. 'And
I really must get going, my dear; goodbye!' He curved
one of his big hands around his wife's cheek with touching gentleness, then bent and kissed her mouth. 'I won't
be late,' he promised, and it occurred to Chiara as she
saw him that whatever the circumstances of their marriage, and whatever her faults, Colin Roberts loved his
wife.

It was an oddly comforting thought as she left the
room with him, although she couldn't have said why.
Campbell was already part way to the front door, impatient to be gone, and Chiara kept pace with her uncle
as they crossed the hall, glancing at him from the corner
of her eye before she ventured to say anything.

'I—I'm sorry Aunt Margaret doesn't like me being
here, Uncle Colin, although I do understand why. The
fact that I'm Italian is only part of the trouble, I know,
but I will try and remember to use English and not
Italian.' She gave him a big warm smile when he stood
back to let her go through the door ahead of him. 'As
a matter of fact Campbell has already mentioned the
fact that it might be more—suitable to call my Scottish
grandfather Grandpa as he does, and I'll try and remember if I'm to stay here for any length of time.'

'My dear child!' Her uncle hugged her close for a
moment, and quite clearly he was affected by her atti-

tude. 'You're very tolerant in the circumstances, and I hope you'll make allowances for both Margaret and Cam. Take my word for it, they're neither of them nearly as inhospitable as they might appear.'

'Oh, but of course they're not,' Chiara hastened to assure him. 'I didn't mean to criticise either of them, because I know exactly how they must be feeling. It must be very hard to accept, after all the work that Campbell has put in, to have a virtual stranger walk in and be handed half of it on a plate.'

Briefly her uncle's kindly blue eyes speculated with a deeper and more shrewd look than she had seen before. 'But you'll not be turning it down?' he said, and she shook her head, wondering if he expected her to do just that.

'I don't think I should, Uncle Colin, do you? You see, if Mamma had lived it would have been hers, and I think she would have wanted me to keep a part of Castle Eyrie. She was sometimes very homesick, you know, even though she loved Italy and she and Papa were idyllically happy.'

'Lovely Marie,' Colin said softly. 'Of course I'm in complete agreement with what Father wants, my dear; Marie was my sister even though we had different mothers, and I loved her dearly. She confessed when she was here on holiday once that she missed Castle Eyrie so much sometimes that she cried, and I know she would have been delighted to know that you and Campbell were to share it.'

'Thank you, Uncle Colin.' Sympathising with his predicament as pig-in-the-middle, Chiara impulsively tiptoed and kissed his cheek, then laughed a little unsteadily when she noticed the Land Rover come into view around the end of the building. 'I'd better go before Campbell starts getting impatient again!'

Leaving her uncle beside his car, she veered left along

the steps. 'Och, never fear about that,' he called after her, with a brief glance at his son's towering length bunched behind the wheel of the Land Rover. 'Cam has all the patience in the world when he wants anything badly enough!'

Chiara had no time to question his meaning, for he turned and got into his car, and when Campbell drew up beside her there was nothing she could do but climb into the vehicle beside him. She gave a brief uneasy glance at a rifle laid along the back seat, but said nothing; countrymen quite often carried guns, she seemed to remember.

'Right?' he asked as she settled into her seat, and receiving a slight nod in reply, he drove off along the track that rose steeply from the public road, then veered off right after a few yards on to an even rougher one.

Chiara did not remember the sheer vastness of the Castle Eyrie estate striking her quite so forcibly before, and it brought home to her just what an enormous task it must be running it. It needed not only cash, and that would be required in plenty, but organisation and sheer hard work too, and she began to see why her aunt looked on her as an interloper, for she had played no part at all in its creation or its upkeep. It was something she would have to give some serious thought to before long, although she had few qualifications that were likely to be of use in running a place like Castle Eyrie.

The forested area alone covered hundred of acres, and that wasn't the full extent by any means. On the other side of the castle the land dropped away sharply and the terrain was all wildly rocky moorland and craggy hills covered with heather and low-growing scrub that seemed to go on for ever. Yet even that, she recalled, was only a fraction of the territory the Roberts had once held in their powerful hands.

Campbell stopped the Land Rover at the edge of the trees, and the moment he stopped the engine the pine-sweet stillness fell about them like a blanket. The air was heavy and there was a curious sense of expectancy, as if something hovered above them, and yet there was an incredible peace too, and it was that which affected Chiara most. She leaned back in her seat and half-closed her eyes, making small dark crescents of shadow on her cheeks.

'It's so incredibly quiet,' she murmured, 'it's almost uncanny.'

'It's ominous,' Campbell declared as he got out of the vehicle, and stood for a moment with both hands on his hips and looking around him. 'There's probably a storm brewing, it's heavy enough.' He didn't offer to help her out, so Chiara helped herself, then stood smoothing down her skirt and looking up at the deep blue sky; wondering what made him anticipate a storm on such a warm, soft morning. 'I saw old Bui Strone over the crags first thing too,' he went on, 'and that usually means we're in for a storm.'

Chiara lowered the hand that had shaded her eyes and frowned at him curiously. 'Old who?'

A hint of mockery gleamed in his eyes for a moment. 'Bui Strone,' he repeated, sounding the 'r' like a miniature drum roll. 'Have you not the Gaelic, girl?'

'No, and neither have you, or you'd have used it to confuse me before now!' Chiara retorted. She moved up alongside him and again put a hand to shade her eyes, searching the area for some clue to his meaning.

'You'll not see him this side of the hill,' Campbell told her. 'I'll take you round on to the moors later and we might get a look at him. Then you can boast that you've actually seen a golden eagle, and there's few enough can do that nowadays.'

'Is that what it means?' She lowered her hand and looked at him. 'If you'd used English I'd have known what you were talking about.'

Smiling faintly, he leaned in and lifted the rifle from

the back of the Land Rover, then took her arm, steer-
ing her into the shadow of the trees. 'You'd have been no
wiser if I'd translated it,' he told her. 'It means old yellow
nose; not very respectful, I agree, but appropriate.'

A few feet in from the edge of the tree belt their way
was barred by a fine steel mesh fence, curved inward at
the top and with a high gate of the same mesh giving
access to whatever lay beyond. Tucking the rifle under
one arm, Campbell unlocked the gate, then carefully
locked it again behind them, and while he was doing it
Chiara was taking stock; looking around her.

The wood smelled strongly of pine and some animal
smell that she couldn't identify, but which made her
wrinkle her nose. It made her vaguely uneasy when she
saw a notice on the gate that said *Danger—Entrance
Strictly Forbidden*, but she concluded that it must have
been put there mostly to deter the visiting public from
going where they were not wanted. Campbell would
hardly have come strolling through there if there was
really any danger, although he did carry a rifle.

The place seemed alive with sounds and movement,
and yet so far she had seen nothing beyond a glimpse
of dark fur up in one of the pine trees. 'A polecat,' said
Campbell, noticing Chiara's glance. 'They've come along
fine since they moved in.'

'You'd never know that fence was there among the
trees,' she ventured as they made their way deeper into
the forest, and he nodded, as if he appreciated the remark.

'That's what we aimed for,' he told her. 'As little
fencing as possible and a natural blending with the
environment as far as it could be managed. That's why
the fence is in a little from the edge of the trees, it makes
it less obvious.'

'Is the outside fenced in the same way?' she asked. 'I
didn't notice anything when we arrived.'

'You'd not see anything that end,' Campbell told her. 'There's no fear of anything straying when food is as plentiful as it is here, and most animals know when they're well off. It's a wee bit different with these laddies, of course; we have to comply with certain safety regulations even though they'd not harm anyone unless they were attacked. There!'

He spoke quietly and following his pointing finger Chiara found herself looking at what appeared to be a group of large Alsatian dogs with small sharp eyes and thick grey fur. Seeing them, the animals paused for a moment, then turned as one and slunk away into the shelter of the trees again. Her heart was thudding hard and panic prickled her scalp as she stood staring at the spot for several seconds after the animals had gone, her mouth suddenly dry.

'What—what were they?' she whispered, and Campbell looked down at her, his vivid blue eyes glinting in the dancing shadows among the trees.

'Wolves, of course,' he said, and Chiara felt the colour drain from her face. 'Och, come on now,' he teased her, 'they were most of them born in captivity, and anyway, they're the most cowardly creatures in the world. Did you not see the way they slunk off when they saw us?'

'But—but——'

She took a firm grip on her shaking body and swallowed hard. Her legs felt almost too weak to support her, and her palms were wet and sticky, as Campbell discovered when he reached and took her hand. His strong fingers clasped hers hard and he eyed her for a moment speculatively. 'They'll not hurt you,' he assured her, and presumably expected his word to be enough.

'You have a notice up warning the public to keep out,' she pointed out in a voice that was little more than a husky whisper, 'and you carry a gun; you *must* think they're dangerous.'

'I carry a gun because I'm not a complete fool,' Campbell told her, 'but I've never yet had to use it. If they were hungry they might have a go, but these fellows *aren't* hungry, and I come in here most days to check on some young ones we think are around somewhere.'

'But—wolves! Everyone knows they're dangerous.'

'No more than the two-legged variety!' He showed his own strong teeth in a smile that mocked her nervousness. 'I'd have thought you were used to wolves, Chiara, a girl like you, living in Italy. Have you never had your bottom pinched? I thought it was a national pastime in your country!'

Chiara jerked her hand free with such violence she almost unbalanced herself. 'At least that's more friendly than walking someone into a den of wild animals!' she retorted. She would like to have stalked off and left him, but in the circumstances she was dependent on him to see her safely out of the compound; and she didn't trust him enough to take it for granted if she stalked off.

He watched her face for a moment and it was hard to read those shadowed eyes. 'If you're scared of being gobbled up by the big bad wolf, I'd best see you safely out,' he said.

Chiara merely nodded, for words were suddenly hard to find, but how she managed to walk back as far as the gate she never knew. At any moment she expected to feel the snarling pack at their heels and she kept a wary eye on their rear, a fact that Campbell noted and mocked her for. Never before had she felt so chillingly afraid as she had back there, and the first thing she did when they emerged from the compound was to put her hands to her mouth while she recovered her composure.

'Chiara?'

He spoke her name surprisingly softly and she noticed that he had disposed of the rifle into the back of the vehicle again. But by then reaction was setting in and she was angry; not only with him, but at her own near-panic a moment since. 'You took me in there deliberately to—to try and scare me!' she accused, trying hard to steady her voice. 'I suppose you thought it was funny trying to frighten me to death!'

'What?' He looked so frankly incredulous that it was hard to believe he could be pretending. 'Oh, don't be so daft, girl!'

He held both her arms as she faced him and his eyes were narrowed and curious, regarding her steadily for a moment, while Chiara kept her gaze on the top button of his shirt because she simply didn't feel up to meeting his eyes. Also there was something oddly distracting about the vee of tanned flesh at the neck of his shirt that helped to dispel her fears.

'Chiara!' A big hand lifted her chin and obliged her to look instead at his mouth. 'You don't honestly believe that!' he declared softly.

'I—I'm not sure what to believe about you,' she said, then raised her head sharply when the sound of his laughter startled her.

His hands spanned her soft throat and for a moment he squeezed gently, then he laughed again, although she suspected there was more anger than amusement in his eyes. 'God, you're a little fool!' he declared, and pulled her into his arms so suddenly that she had no oppor-tunity to do anything about it. 'You really do believe I'm capable of anything!'

Chiara experienced another flick of panic when he tightened his hold until she was crushed against him so hard she could feel every muscle in the body that throbbed with life under her flat, defensive palms. His mouth on hers was ruthlessly forceful so that she made a small protesting sound just before her lips parted as if of their own accord, and her eyes closed to shut out the sight of that fierce dark face.

It was a questing, exploratory kiss but stunningly affecting, and when she found herself free of it suddenly she stepped back quickly and would have moved out of reach, but strong fingers checked her and spun her back in front of him. She was breathing hard and when she looked up at him briefly, her eyes were huge and lustrous but still slightly dazed.

'What are you running away from?' Campbell demanded.

She tugged ineffectually at her arm. 'Let me go, Campbell!'

He laid the back of one hand lightly over the throbbing beat of her heart and she flinched as from a blow, the rate of her pulse rising swiftly. 'You can't be that afraid of being kissed, surely?' he mused quietly. 'Do you always run when you're kissed; or are you making an exception of me?'

'Stop it!' Chiara told him breathlessly. 'Stop trying to —to goad me, Campbell!'

She actually managed to slip from his grasp for a second or two, but she had taken no more than a single step towards freedom before he was beside her again and his hand around her arm, his long fingers stroking her soft skin lightly until she drew away from him again. In a brief glance she noticed how his eyes were gleaming in that teak-dark face, and she wished she had the strength of mind to simply walk off.

'Don't tell me you've never been kissed before!' he said. 'I won't—I *can't* believe that!'

'Not—not like that,' she insisted, shrugging uneasily.

She wanted nothing more than to get away from him, but her swift glance up the hill towards the castle must have told him what she had in mind, and he sought to delay her further. 'How was it different, Chiara?'

The probing was gentle but relentless, and she felt a curious sense of helplessness as she stood there facing him. Swallowing hard, she tried not to let her pulse respond so urgently to the gentle stroking fingers on her arm, for it was much too disturbing. 'For—for one thing because you're my cousin,' she told him in a light breathless voice. 'I—I'm not sure it's right that you should kiss me like that when we're cousins.'

'For heaven's sake, why not?'

His puzzlement was seemingly genuine, and she did not understand her own reluctance to leave him now that she had the opportunity. But she had never before been so affected by any man as she seemed to be by Campbell Roberts, and she found the experience vaguely alarming.

'What's wrong with cousins kissing?' he asked, and she glanced up for a moment from the corner of her eye. 'Or do you think you're too young for me, is that it, Chiara?' He laughed shortly and she felt herself flinch from it. 'Are you putting me firmly in my place, pretty cousin, because you feel you're too young for someone like me?'

'Of course I'm not too young——' She let her objection hang fire because she realised what it could get her into, and Campbell was shaking his head.

'Och, you're a daft little devil! We're not closely enough related for there to be anything taboo about me kissing you!'

'Close enough!'

'Hah!'

His expressive snort of derision brought a flush of colour to her cheeks because it was accompanied by a sweeping gesture with one big hand that dismissed any reason he chose not to recognise. It was typical of him, Chiara decided, to simply dismiss anything that was likely to impede his own desires, and she glanced again up the steep hill. He had told his mother that when she had had enough she could find her own way back; and she had just about had enough.

'I'm going back,' she told him in a slightly unsteady

voice, and she was already starting the climb when he called after her.

'It's no use you running away from me,' he said, and his deep, quiet voice had remarkable clarity on the quiet hillside. 'I mean to marry you eventually!'

Chiara nearly lost her balance when she swung round to look at him, and his faintly sardonic smile made her draw a swift breath and clench her hands tightly. 'Never!' she declared. 'Never, never, never!'

Chiara said nothing to either her uncle or her grandfather about Campbell's staggeringly unexpected pronouncement, partly because she could not bring herself to believe he had meant it; how could she in the circumstances? And yet there were reasons enough why he would see it as desirable, she recognised, not least because by marrying her he would ensure that Castle Eyrie and its lands remained intact, and that he had control over it in its entirety.

She could even see his point to some extent, but it made no difference to her abhorrence of the idea. Because Aunt Margaret had brought social advancement to her ambitious father by obediently marrying the local laird's son. Chiara saw no reason to follow her example just so that Campbell could get his hands on the whole of their grandfather's property instead of only half of it.

She had been there a fairly uneventful couple of weeks when, as he had promised, Campbell offered to drive her over the moor in the hope of spotting the elusive golden eagle he was so proud of. It was a rarity, she knew, and he was rightly pleased to have one nesting on their land, but she was less deeply involved than he was in preservation of his country's wild life, and so far she could not share his boundless enthusiasm, although she could understand it to some degree.

After the episode of taking her into the wolf enclosure,

she was rather surprised that he had asked her to go with him again, and she pondered on the enigma of the man as she went out to join him in response to a blast on the Land Rover's horn. He was doing something under the bonnet of the vehicle and she noticed how he had to bend almost double to see what he was doing, because of his height.

He was wearing brown cords and half-boots with a fawn shirt that was carelessly fastened to show a long vee of tanned flesh in the opening—a lean sombre figure except for his red-gold hair, and when she looked across at him while she came down the front steps, Chiara felt those curious little trickles run along her spine again at the sight of him. Her eyes hastily evasive when he looked up and saw her.

'Hop in,' he invited. 'I'll just be a minute.'

'Something wrong?' She wondered what would happen if the Land Rover's engine failed when they were miles from anywhere. From what she had seen of Campbell so far she thought he was most likely to put her afoot to go for help while he stayed with the vehicle, and she did not fancy that idea at all.

'Just a wee bit murmur that I'm not altogether happy about,' he told her. 'It'll be fine soon enough, don't worry.' He peered at her around the edge of the raised bonnet and his eyes gleamed with speculation. 'If the engine gives out I'd hate you to suspect me of evil intent, and you would, wouldn't you, Chiara?'

It followed too closely on her own speculation for her to deny it, and instead she chose not to say anything at all, but climbed into the vehicle and sat quietly while he finished whatever he was doing. It clearly hadn't been very serious, for he slammed down the bonnet only a few moments later and glanced at her briefly as he slid on to the seat.

'Do you never wear trousers?' he asked, as the vehicle

moved off, and Chiara looked round at him curiously.

'Very seldom,' she said. 'Nonno Manti was very traditional and he didn't like women to wear trousers; he lived with us for most of my life.' She looked down at her slim legs below a green cotton skirt and frowned slightly. 'If you think I should change, I do have a pair of trousers I could put on.'

'Not for me,' Campbell assured her with a quick grin. 'I'm a leg man myself, like your Italian grandpappy! I just thought you might be more—comfortable in trousers, that's all.' The way he used one big hand when he said it would have done credit to any one of her countrymen and the colour came swiftly into her cheeks. 'Climbing rocks isn't often done in skirts these days, but if you don't mind, I'm sure I don't.'

Chiara was convinced that he had gone out of his way to try and embarrass her, and her temper began to rise at the thought of him being so determinedly provocative. 'It would have been more to the point if you'd mentioned it before we left the house,' she told him. 'But I warn you I'm not very good on heights, so I shan't be climbing *too* far up anywhere. I thought we were going to watch for this eagle of yours flying, I didn't realise I was expected to go calling on him personally!'

From the time he took to reply, she suspected her response was not quite what he expected, and it gave her a moment of satisfaction. 'Did you not want to come?' he asked, as if he found it hard to believe, then went on at once to decry the idea. 'Och, but of course you did, no one would pass up a chance like this!'

Chiara eyed him for a moment through her lashes. He was an enthusiast, and there was something oddly affecting about his feeling for the ruggedly beautiful countryside and its wealth of wild life. 'Yes of course I wanted to come,' she said, 'I shouldn't be here otherwise. I don't quite understand your complete devotion to your animals and birds, but I think—I think I might in time.'

'I hope so!' Campbell declared feelingly. 'When Grandpa's gone I'd hate to think of Castle Eyrie being hacked up to provide you with enough cash to shoot off back to Italy and live the life of Riley!'

'So that's why you made that—that ridiculous remark the other day about marrying me!'

He glanced at her briefly. 'Was it ridiculous?' he challenged, the soft burr of his voice sliding like a gentle finger along her spine.

'It would have been simpler just to offer to buy my half from me,' Chiara pointed out, although she knew full well she would never part with it, whatever the circumstances. It was, she felt, her mother's birthright as well as hers.

'Can't afford it,' Campbell informed her with unexpected frankness. 'That's why I decided to marry you; it's the perfect solution, and you'd not be sorry, I promise you.'

Something in those vivid blue eyes when they were turned on her for a moment made her catch her breath, and her heart thudded wildly in a way that made her despair for her common sense. '*You* might be very sorry indeed,' she warned. 'I may be a good thirteen years younger than you are, Campbell, but I'm not the meek little schoolgirl I was when you saw me last, and you don't frighten me any more!'

'I wasn't intending to frighten you,' Campbell assured her quietly, 'just—tame you a little.'

'You——'

'Do you remember the loch?' His question broke smoothly across her objection and he turned the Land Rover off the track and took it across the heather tussocks, bumping and bouncing to the very edge of the big loch. 'Did Grandpa ever bring you here?'

She looked at the broad expanse of dark water, seemingly bottomless and so still that not even the light breeze stirred its surface. When he cut the engine she was again assailed by that same sense of peace; the feeling that made her half-close her eyes and relax completely for a second or two.

'I remember coming a couple of times,' she replied in answer to his query, and struggled to recall the name her grandfather had told her. 'Loch—Dew.'

'Loch Dhu.' He corrected her pronunciation as he got out of the vehicle, and Chiara accepted the correction just as she had done when her grandfather had done exactly the same thing some years before. 'Did he ever tell you anything about it?' he asked, and she shook her head.

He was looking at her as if he sought confirmation of her interest, and Chiara was nothing loath to admit she was interested. 'Has it got a history?' she asked, by way of encouragement.

'Some.' He set one booted foot on one of the round white rocks that bordered the loch, and gazed narrow-eyed at the dark, still water. 'In Gaelic the name means dark loch, but it isn't only from its colour that it got its name. It's supposed to have been an ordinary grey-blue at one time, until one of our disreputable ancestors stole himself a bride from a neighbouring clan. The lady was betrothed to a very powerful laird who took exception to being deprived of his prize, and he set off with his kinsmen to take her back. Unfortunately by the time he and his men got here it was too late and her innocence was no longer intact, to put it politely. Rather than leave her with her Roberts lover, he took her with him, but stopped on his way back and threw her into the loch, where she drowned. Ever since then the water has been as dark as it is now.'

'Poor girl!'

Campbell gave her a small and somewhat mocking smile. 'Aye, well, women weren't as important in those

days as they are now and our hero found himself another wife. I dare say she would have got a pretty rough
time of it either way.'

'Well, thank goodness we can expect something better
nowadays!' Chiara retorted. 'And if you told me that
tale with the hope of scaring me into marrying you or
else, Campbell, you needn't have bothered!'

He surveyed her narrowly for a moment. 'You'd
sooner go into the loch?' he asked.

'I'd sooner go into the loch!' she retorted.

His laughter was completely unexpected, and also
curiously affecting as he stood with his head thrown
back and his blue eyes gleaming, showing his strong
teeth in a way that put her in mind of his precious
wolves. 'Oh, I've no intention of throwing you into the
loch,' he promised, and reached out to stroke one long
finger lightly round the curve of her cheek and down her
neck. 'I've much better things to do with a girl like you
than drown her!'

Chiara could feel herself trembling like a leaf, and her
anger was as much for her own impressionability as for
his brashness, for she could not deny that she responded
to him in a way she never had to any man before. Sum-
moning all her self-possession, she lifted her chin and
looked at him, her near-black eyes glowing darkly in her
small face.

'If we've come to see your precious eagle, where is
he?' she demanded, but her gaze slid away when he
looked directly at her. 'You can try any tactics you like,'
she went on a little breathlessly, 'but it won't make a
scrap of difference—I won't marry you!'

'We'll see!'

A certain look in his eyes brought sudden urgency to
her pulse, and she deliberately turned away from him to
scan the light blue summer sky. 'Where is that bird supposed to appear—if it does?'

He was silent for a moment and Chiara could guess

that he was not accustomed to being rebuffed quite so determinedly. Then she heard a faint click of his boot heels on the pebbles and he was immediately behind her. 'Over there!' he drew her against him so that he could better direct her gaze, and pointed a finger as he brought his face down close beside hers, the roughness of his cheek pressed close for a moment. 'Over beyond that crag, do you see him?'

Something of his pride and pleasure thrilled through her own body as she was drawn to him, and she lifted her eyes to find the dark, majestic creature that hovered above the heathery moorland. Whether or not it was because of Campbell that she was so affected, she didn't know for sure, but his hard fingers dug deep into her shoulders and she instinctively leaned back until his body seemed to curve about her while her eyes remained fixed on the soaring eagle.

'Does—does that mean it's going to storm again?' she asked, noting the creature's location. 'Didn't you say he warns you when there's going to be a storm?'

'He's mebbe not always right,' Campbell allowed, and she sensed that he was smiling. 'But by God, he's always worth watching!'

The warm flutter of his breathing tingled on her skin like a caress and her senses soared like the flight of the eagle as she stood enfolded by his vigorous warmth. 'He's magnificent,' she murmured, and again Campbell spoke close to her ear.

'Aye, he's magnificent, and no one can touch him!' She felt rather than saw him turn slightly and it was automatic to look up at him by tilting back her head and looking over her shoulder. 'Though some would like to!' he added, half under his breath, and she frowned.

'But who would want to?' He inclined his head in a brusque nod and she followed its direction. Right over on the horizon was a man in a parked jeep, a hazy figure that was for the moment unmoving, and she thought he had a hand to his eyes as if he too followed the flight of the eagle. 'Who is it, Campbell?'

'A neighbour.' The information, she guessed, was grudgingly given, and there was no mistaking the rasp of harshness in his voice.

Whoever he was the man was moving again, along the skyline, and she turned back to see the great bird she had been watching dive swiftly down towards the heather. 'He's got something!'

'Breakfast,' Campbell observed dryly. 'The eyrie's up there on that crag and he has hungry mouths to feed, but God help him if he's taken another of Gavin Mc-Donald's lambs. He'll be out with his gun after him, whether or no he stands to get jailed for it!'

'You mean—it takes lambs?'

'That's right,' Campbell agreed, and something in his eyes mocked her obvious distaste. 'Those wee woolly things with long tails! To an eagle a weak lamb is fair game, and it was the farmers who practically exterminated them in the first place.'

'With reason, surely,' Chiara claimed, unsure which to side with.

Campbell's hands still rested on her shoulders and with her head turned as it was, her view of those vivid blue eyes was more intimate and close than it had ever been before. 'So you'd kill off old Bui Strone, would you?' he challenged.

Nor did she want that, Chiara realised, and came face to face for the first time with one of the problems of conservation. 'I just wish there was some way of—I don't know; making things work.'

'Have your cake and eat it too, you mean?' Campbell teased, and his face hovered above hers, too close for comfort. 'No one's worked out a way of doing that yet, so I keep trying to keep some of the wilder creatures safe, and Gavin McDonald keeps trying to get rid of them. It's an ongoing battle and I doubt *we'll* see an end of it.'

'Do you want to?'

Heaven knew what had possessed her to ask him that, for it was so unmistakably a challenge and Campbell was not a man to back off from a challenge. His eyes gleamed down at her for a moment, then he turned her within the circle of his arms to face him, drawing her close again so that she was pressed to the long lean length of him and stunningly conscious of that irresistible maleness that attracted her despite herself.

'I enjoy a good fight,' he admitted, his mouth showing a ghost of a smile, 'I admit it, especially when it's for something I want badly enough.' His head came down to her and the hard pressure of his arms held her immovable while his mouth sought hers. 'You'll give me a bonny fight, won't you, Chiara?' he murmured, a second before he stopped her from replying.

It did not occur to her, after the first second of instinctive struggle, to do anything about him kissing her, and her body seemed to mould itself naturally to the hard lines of his. Not until he nuzzled his warm mouth to her neck did she feel a flutter of warning that brought her suddenly, almost reluctantly, back to her senses.

Struggling against the enfolding arms, she fought to free herself, and took an involuntary step backwards when he eased his hold on her suddenly. Brushing her hands down her skirt was designed only to give her time to recover, and she could feel the intensity of his gaze as he stood watching her.

She straightened up suddenly and walked across to the Land Rover, and it was a second or two before Campbell followed her. Climbing in beside her, he started the engine, then glanced at her from the corner of his eye. His soft chuckle startled her, as his laughter always did, and she kept her hands tightly clenched on her lap while he started the vehicle moving back on to the track.

'You told me I could try any tactics I liked,' he reminded her, and Chiara remembered, ruefully, that she had indeed done just that.

CHAPTER THREE

CHIARA had tried to avoid being alone with Campbell as far as possible during the following week or so; not simply because she anticipated another scene like the one by the loch, but because she wasn't sure enough of her own powers of resistance where he was concerned. She had seen him on and off for years from the time she was a baby until seven years ago, but whatever she had felt about him then was nothing like the effect he seemed to have on her now. She saw each and every move he made as an attempt to persuade her to the idea of marrying him, and that she was firmly set against in the circumstances.

It wasn't easy to avoid him either, for he very often suggested that she accompany him on what he referred to as his rounds, and he seemed quite prepared to abandon his customary mode to travel and use the Land Rover instead of the horse he more normally rode. In the event it made it even harder to resist when he was so ready to adapt.

Although she did not readily admit it yet, she was becoming more interested in his scheme to re-establish some of Scotland's ancient wild life, even if she did take a wary view of some of the more dangerous species. She was still cautious about going near the wolf compound, but she was beginning to feel something of their fascination, even if it was inspired by a lingering primitive fear of their reputation.

Campbell's claim of being unable to induce anyone to come and live and work in such an isolated environment prompted Chiara to offer her help, although she had no idea just what she could do. 'You mean it?' he asked, and gave her a swift sideways glance as he drove the Land Rover down the track to the wooded section.

Chiara hoped she hadn't been too rash, making the offer, but she could always turn down anything she felt unable to cope with. 'I'd like to do something,' she told him, 'and if you're short-handed as you say——'

'You're staying on, then?'

It wasn't the response she expected, and Chiara frowned. 'I promised Grandpa I would,' she reminded him. 'For a while anyway.'

He nodded, and his apparent satisfaction, although unvoiced, rather surprised her. 'Do you drive?'

'A little; I'm not an expert, but I've driven at home, though always with someone in the car with me.'

'No good to me,' Campbell told her shortly. 'If I have to come with you I might as well drive myself.' She was about to object to his attitude, but he went on, bouncing the Land Rover down the deeply rutted track as if he was testing its stamina as well as theirs. 'On second thoughts,' he said, 'we get very little traffic around here, and it'll not matter if you run a few rabbits over as long as you make it there and back in one piece. What about a licence?'

'I have a driving licence, if that's what you mean.'

'That's good enough. If you come to grief and Charlie Houston hauls you in to the local pokey, well——' He looked pointedly at her slim rounded figure and softly flushed face, and smiled. 'Just give him a look with your big black eyes and wiggle that sexy little shape and he'll not be too hard on you.'

Chiara's flush grew even more pronounced and she eyed him reproachfully while she clung to the side of the vehicle rather than be thrown against him yet again. 'You have a very distorted view of the Italian way of life,' she told him. 'The other week you implied that all

Italian men are wolves, and now you're suggesting that the women are hip-swinging sirens! We're just people —like anyone else.'

'Except that some *are* hip-swinging little sirens,' Campbell insisted as he braked the vehicle to a halt. When they had stopped he half-turned in his seat to face her and his eyes took stock of her flushed and faintly rebellious face for a moment. '*Will* you work for me, Chiara?' he asked. 'I can find enough for you to do, you know, though it'll not be all driving.'

'I'll help,' she stressed firmly. 'I shan't be working *for* you.'

'If that's how you want to say it,' he agreed, unexpectedly amenable.

His proximity was always disturbing, and never more so than now. There was a certain arrogant, untamed air about him that affected her more than she cared to admit, and it made her feel very small and vulnerable, especially when he stroked a long forefinger lightly down her cheek. As she shifted slightly, out of his reach, she noticed Murdoch, his one assistant, approaching from behind, and she silently thanked heaven for his coming.

'Mr Murdoch's coming,' she said, and Campbell half-turned his head to glance at the man over his shoulder, then he very deliberately leaned forward and kissed her lightly on her mouth. 'Och, Murdoch's a man of the world,' he told her facetiously, 'he'll not die of shock from seeing me kiss a pretty girl.'

'I suppose he's seen you do it too often to be shocked!' Chiara suggested, then turned quickly when he laughed, and got out.

Campbell swung his long legs out, then stood the other side of the Land Rover looking at her for a moment, and it was hard to decide whether it was resentment or amusement that accounted for the gleam in his eyes. 'You're right,' he agreed unhesitatingly.

'Though my tastes usually run to redheads, not brunettes.'

'Then you'd better marry one of *them*!'

There was still a glimmer of something in his eyes, but his mouth had a firm determined look. 'Oh no, my lovely,' he denied. 'You're the girl for me, and no matter how hard you fight me, I'll bring you round to my way of thinking one way or another!'

'Not if I decide to go back to Italy, you won't!' she declared, and just for a moment there was a glint of speculation there.

'You'll not do that,' he said, after a moment or two. 'Not when you've promised Grandpa you'll stay; and you confirmed it to me not five minutes since. Now, do you still feel like helping me or not?' It was a direct challenge and Chiara felt a thrill of response from her all too responsive emotions.

'Of course I'll help,' she told him, keeping a firm hold on her rather unsteady voice. 'I want to make this business as successful as possible, and then when I get my half of it I can ask a good price and live for the rest of my life on the proceeds!'

'You little——'

She laughed a little breathlessly and her fingers curled tightly over the edge of the door when he took a threatening half-step forward. 'What do you want me to do first, Campbell?'

'Watch your step!' he retorted.

But Murdoch's short, stocky figure was almost upon them, and the man's sharp senses had probably already detected the crackling, volatile atmosphere, although he could not have heard any of it. There was no time to take it further and Campbell recovered himself quickly. Lifting the inevitable rifle from the back seat, he stood for a moment; while he decided how best to make use of her, Chiara guessed.

'Can you handle this thing?' he asked, indicating the Land Rover, and she eyed it for a moment uncertainly.

'I can try,' she decided. 'Where do you want me to take it?'

'Only as far as the village, to Houston's farm.'

'The same name——' she began, and he nodded.

'The police station, the garage and the farm are all manned by Ian Houston's brood. Old Ian has a load of feed for me that I promised I'd fetch this morning. If you keep to the road that leads down to the loch-side, you can't miss it. Can you manage that O.K.?'

'Of course!'

Chiara got back into the Land Rover and slid behind the wheel. 'Oh—and, Chiara!' She looked at him, stopped in mid-stride and turned to face her. 'Tell the old man that if he gets you humping that stuff I'll see he never gets paid for it!'

She was still smiling to herself as she drove across the bumpy hillside to the public road, and having successfully got as far as driving on the smoother surface she thought she could afford to relax a little. It wasn't strictly true to say that she quarrelled with Campbell, but there were all too many occasions when they both became more impassioned than the subject warranted; and the incidents always disturbed her in a way that didn't quite make sense.

She had teased him with the possibility of her going back to Italy, but in fact she had already sent for most of her belongings, and she had no intention of breaking the promise she had made her grandfather. But it was no bad thing, she decided, to keep a man like Campbell Roberts in suspense, whether or not she meant it.

The road down to the village was steep and winding, and she was not paying as much attention as she should have been to her driving, taking account of the fact that she was driving not only a strange vehicle but in a strange country too. In fact she had not yet realised that she was driving on the right-hand side of the road when she was forced to jump hastily on the brake.

The man she had so nearly collided with had jumped to safety in the same moment that she came to a screeching halt, but it had been much too close for comfort. Shaken by the near miss and accustomed to the volatile and instant reaction of her own countrymen in such a situation, Chiara did not hesitate to express her fright and anger in voluble Italian. It did not even occur to her that she would be incomprehensible, and the look on the man's face suggested that the sound of a foreign tongue startled him as much or more than her unexpected appearance on the wrong side of the road.

He stared at her for several moments, while Chiara sat with her head bent and her forehead resting on her arms. Recovering her wits, she began to realise whose fault it had been, and her scrutiny of her victim was instinctive rather than deliberate, as she tried to guess what his reaction was going to be.

He was medium height and sandy-haired, as far as she could see, and he was quite good-looking, with hazel eyes that regarded her steadily now that he had recovered from his surprise. He had a sporting gun, correctly broken, tucked under one arm and he looked rather alarmingly serious about it all as he approached her.

Chiara knew she was blushing and she gnawed anxiously on her lip, wondering what on earth she was going to say; but in the event it was he who apologised. 'I beg your pardon,' he said, touching the brim of the tweed hat he wore. 'I wasn't looking where I was going, and you came on me unexpectedly.' He had a certain austere look, for all that his eyes showed a definite appreciation, and something seemed to occur to him suddenly. 'Er—do you speak any English?'

'Oh yes—yes, I do.'

Chiara was remembering what Campbell had said about her running foul of the local law, but she trembled to think what he was going to say about it happening so soon. It shocked her rather to realise that she was actually considering his suggestion that she should charm her way out of it, and she told herself that the smile she gave the man with the gun was merely friendly and polite and not in the least seductive.

'I'm *very* sorry I cursed you, in the circumstances.'

'Did you?' His good-looking face showed only relief that she spoke English, and he did not even respond to her smile. His voice had the soft Highland accent, just as Campbell's did, but was more pronounced. 'That was Spanish, wasn't it?' he asked. 'Or Italian?'

'Italian,' Chiara said, and proffered a hand, still hoping to coax a smile from him. 'My name is Chiara Manti, and I can't say how sorry I am that this happened. I was day-dreaming and I didn't remember I was driving on the wrong side of the road.'

He took her hand and shook it briefly, but for the moment he didn't offer his own name, and he seemed much more interested in the Land Rover she was driving than anything else. 'This is a Castle Eyrie vehicle, isn't it?' he asked, and Chiara nodded, wondering who he could be.

'That's right—Mr Ian Roberts is my grandfather.'

He frowned, but nevertheless belatedly introduced himself. 'I'm Gavin McDonald; you'll no doubt have heard of me from your cousin.'

It took Chiara a second or two to remember where she had heard the name before, and then she remembered the solitary figure in the jeep that she and Campbell had seen that day beside the loch. If Campbell was to be believed the man was no friend of his, and was completely out of sympathy with his scheme for restocking the locality with wildlife. A sheep-farmer was how Campbell described him.

'I think Campbell did mention you,' she acknowledged cautiously. 'We saw you one day when we were watching for the golden eagle.'

'Murderous brute!' His vehemence startled her briefly, and his hazel eyes regarded her as if he suspected she was completely out of sympathy with his feelings. 'But you'll be in favour of that wilderness they're trying to create, no doubt,' he guessed. 'I suppose you've been brought in to help take care of the menace that could deprive folk of their livelihood!'

Chiara understood how his battle with Campbell could have built up over the years and she sympathised to some extent, but she disliked his taking it for granted that she was a party to any harassment of the local people. 'My grandfather asked me to stay with him, and I offered to lend Campbell a hand, that's all,' she told him, keeping her resentment well concealed. 'I'm afraid I'm not familiar enough with either side of the argument to be sure which I support, Mr McDonald, although it must be heartbreaking to lose your lambs to old Bui Strone.'

'The eagle?' She nodded. 'It isn't only the damned bird,' he insisted, obviously relishing the idea of an audience for his grievances, 'it's the idea of having a pack of wolves roaming around up there! My whole flock could go overnight if those brutes got out!'

'Oh, but they won't,' Chiara assured him earnestly. 'They're very securely fenced in, Mr McDonald, and Campbell is very strict about always locking the compound each time he goes in and out. I can assure you that there's no danger at all of them escaping.'

'You're very comforting, Miss Manti.'

Whether or not he was influenced by what she had told him, she chose to think he was, and it was in keeping with her natural impulsiveness when she placed a hand on his arm, though quite obviously the gesture startled him. 'Please believe me,' she pleaded.

Something in his expression changed, and she detected a slightly more aware look in his eyes as he looked down at the hand on his arm. Then he quite openly took stock of her with a glimmer of expression that gave lie to the sobriety of his manner. 'I hope your stay is to be a long one, Miss Manti—may we hope it will be?'

Convinced she had made progress, Chiara smiled. 'I'll be here for several months anyway,' she told him.

'That's a pleasant prospect indeed.'

Coming from such a sober man she felt the compliment was all the more sincere, and she had already decided that she liked Gavin McDonald, whatever Campbell's feelings were towards him, or his towards Campbell. But she had still her errand to do and Campbell, she imagined, would not be a patient man in any circumstances.

'I have to go,' she said, starting the engine. 'But may I stress again how sorry I am for what happened, Mr McDonald.'

'Och no, no!' The soft voice soothed her, and as if by accident his hand settled over hers where it rested on the door. 'I do hope to see you again, Miss Manti, before very long. Goodbye now.'

Thinking about Campbell's sworn enemy kept her preoccupied even after she had collected the feed from the farm and was on her way back to the castle with it, and she hoped there would be a chance to meet Gavin McDonald again. She hesitated, however, to mention the meeting to Campbell, and it was only because he questioned a slight dent in the side of the Land Rover that she told him. It must have happened when she swerved into the bank to avoid running down Gavin McDonald.

He showed no resentment of their meeting, but rather seemed to find it vaguely amusing that the farmer had stopped and talked to her. 'It's not like him to stand and yammer to a lassie,' he claimed, with a smile that suggested he found his neighbour sadly lacking in that direction too. 'It must have been your big beautiful eyes, lass.' Sliding a hand under her hair, he stroked her neck lightly, as if he mused on the situation. 'But I'm surprised even you could coax him out of reporting you when he discovered who you were.'

'I wasn't trying to coax him out of anything,' Chiara denied, ignoring the fact that she had toyed with the idea for a while. 'He's a nice man, and he understood that I was sorry for what happened.' It was irresistible to go on as she did, and she watched his face from the corner of her eye. 'In fact I hope to see him again, so don't be too surprised if I date your public enemy number one, will you?'

The fingers on her neck tightened suddenly, and she protested, jerking her head free of their grip. 'You would too, wouldn't you?' Campbell guessed. His eyes were shadowed by their long lashes so that it was hard to see what his expression was, and his mouth showed a hint of a smile, albeit a tight and vaguely menacing one that stirred uneasy tremors in her. 'You'd date Gavin McDonald just for the sheer hell of it if you thought it would get at me!'

'I'd date him because he's nice and I happen to like him!' Chiara declared. 'And because whatever you say, I still have a will of my own and can pick and choose who I got out with!'

'Come out with me!'

It was so abrupt and unexpected that Chiara said nothing for a moment, only stood with her eyes lifted to the firm line of his mouth and shivering with some inner sensation she could not begin to identify. Then she passed her tongue over her lips and raised her eyes just long enough to see the bright gleaming blueness of his.

'Is—is that an invitation or an ultimatum?' she murmured huskily.

Campbell bent and kissed her forehead; as gentle a caress as he had ever bestowed on her. 'An invitation,' he promised, 'which you're quite at liberty to turn down if you've a mind to.'

And which he knew she would find irresistible, Chiara guessed as she stood with her eyes downcast. 'I won't turn it down,' she promised in the same small husky voice. 'Not if you're asking me for the right reasons, Campbell.' She sensed him frown and glanced upward briefly. 'I don't want you to think I'm weakening about marrying you.'

He slid both hands round her throat, his long fingers under her hair so that he held her face between his big palms, and his thumbs lightly touched her mouth, pulling down the full lower lip. 'You're a very lovely girl and I want to take you out to dinner,' he whispered with his lips close to hers. 'Is that a good enough reason?'

Her heart was thudding violently and for a moment Chiara had forgotten the existence of Gavin McDonald as she lifted her mouth to him. Being kissed by Campbell was becoming a habit, and one she was beginning to acquire a taste for. Just as long as she remembered to keep it firmly in mind that she wasn't going to marry him at any price, she did not see why she shouldn't enjoy it.

Campbell had said nothing more about taking her to dinner, and it occurred to Chiara that perhaps he had simply been playing with her after all; trying to prove that he could persuade her to him just as often as he chose. But meeting again with Gavin McDonald rather precipitated matters as far as he was concerned.

She was once more on an errand for Campbell when she again bumped into Gavin, but in this instance the meeting was less traumatic for both of them. He seemed inclined to stop and talk even longer on this occasion, and his invitation to dinner was not altogether a surprise, she had to admit, although not exactly what she had anticipated.

'We'd love to have you come, Miss Manti,' he told her, 'and there'll be just the three of us, so you'll not be among a lot of strangers, and Robert will be put to bed before dinner.'

It had not occurred to her that Gavin McDonald might be a married man with a family, although it should have done, she realised. Maybe it had been something in the way he looked at her which, although far short of Campbell's bold challenging scrutiny, was meaningful enough to suggest he found her attractive and wanted her to know it. Hence the invitation to dinner with the family; he could hardly invite her out when he had a wife and child.

'Robert's your son?' she speculated, and just for a second Gavin McDonald's eyes narrowed slightly.

'No,' he denied in his soft Highland voice. 'Robert is my sister Betty's son; we share the house.'

'Oh, I see.' It was a relief, Chiara had to admit, and she quite looked forward to her evening out even if it wasn't quite what she had expected. 'But please don't put the little boy to bed on my account,' she begged. 'I like children.'

The gravely good-looking face still did not smile, but there was something in the eyes that she found oddly disconcerting. 'Oh, you'll be meeting him,' he promised. 'He's a fine boy and Betty is aye fond of showing him off. She'll especially like you to see him, Miss Manti.'

Touched by his pride in his young nephew, Chiara

acted impulsively, as she was prone to do all too often. 'Won't you please call me Chiara? It's so much more friendly.'

A hint of a smile touched his straight mouth for a moment, and it was obvious the invitation pleased him. 'Indeed it is,' he agreed, 'so will you not call me Gavin?'

'Gladly!' She smiled, feeling quite pleased with the world at the moment; then she glanced at her watch and pulled a face. 'But I'd better be going or Campbell will think I'm either lost or broken down, and come looking for me.'

'He'll keep a close eye on you, then?' Gavin McDonald suggested softly, and Chiara quite automatically avoided his eyes when she answered.

'He knows I'm rather prone to plunge into things without stopping to think,' she told him, 'and Campbell has a very strong family feeling. He'd concern himself with whether I get into a scrape or not.'

'Like our last meeting,' he reminded her, and somehow Chiara knew he was angling to discover whether or not she had told Campbell about it.

'That simply proved to him that I'm a crazy woman,' she told him with a laugh that made light of Campbell's reaction. 'He'd expect me to drive on the wrong side of the road!' She had no intention of saying any more on the subject and again she consulted her wrist-watch. 'Now I really must go. Thank you, Mr—Gavin, I'll see you tonight!'

'About seven,' he told her, then called after her as she turned away. 'I don't think I'd tell Campbell Roberts that you're coming to the farm if I were you, in view of the way things are.'

Chiara had never been underhand about anything, and she did not like the idea of keeping her visit to the McDonald home a secret. 'I'm not very good at being secretive, Gavin,' she explained, 'and Campbell's opinion doesn't matter one way or the other. I make my own friends.'

She wasn't mistaken, she felt sure. Something very like satisfaction showed in his eyes for a moment, and in view of his suggestion that she keep their dinner date a secret, it didn't make much sense. 'I look forward to seeing you, whatever you decide,' he said, and she smiled.

'I look forward to it too.'

But as she drove back up the hill to Castle Eyrie a short time later, Chiara looked forward a lot less to letting Campbell know just where and in what circumstances she was seeing Gavin McDonald. Eventually she decided on telling no one the full truth, and simply said that she was having dinner with him and left it at that.

'You're a traitor to your family, and to Campbell especially!' was Aunt Margaret's reaction, and even her kindly uncle looked as if he wished she had turned down the invitation.

Her grandfather's view was more difficult to assess, but he did frown and his faded blue eyes regarded her thoughtfully for a moment. 'Just be sure you don't get too involved, girl,' he warned her, and left it at that.

But whatever anyone said, Chiara saw no reason to change her mind, and seven o'clock found her driving along the short farm track to the McDonald house, in the car that Campbell had only very reluctantly loaned her. She was wearing a cream dress that was in striking contrast to her colouring, and she did not altogether understand her almost shivering nervousness as she pulled up outside the front door.

The house looked fairly big, but it had an air of careless untidiness that suggested its occupants were more concerned with practicalities than appearance, and the evening sun made red and gold eyes of the low windows. No one came out when she stopped the car, and she sat

for a moment, willing herself to get out and knock on
the door.

She was standing brushing down her dress when Gavin
McDonald came round from the back of the house.
Seeing her, he gave one of his seemingly rare smiles and
extended a hand in greeting. 'Come away in, Chiara,' he
told her, leading the way back round the house. 'We
never use the front door, and I only just heard your
car.'

'Campbell's car, in fact,' she corrected him, for something to say. He made her feel uneasy and she didn't
quite know why. 'I don't have a car of my own.'

He saw her in through the open door ahead of him,
then took the lead as they passed through a big farmhouse kitchen and went on into another, smaller room
at the front of the house. Its musty closeness suggested
that it was rarely used, and as they walked in a young
woman got up from the armchair she had been sitting in.
The relationship was obvious, but the woman regarded
her more with speculation than welcome, so that Chiara's
first impression was one of chilling assessment.

'This is my sister Betty; Betty, Miss Manti—Chiara.'

They shook hands briefly, and it was a moment or
two before Chiara realised there was a fourth person in
the room. Gavin's sister turned and drew a small boy
from behind her chair, and her eyes were fixed on
Chiara's face with that close, almost cunning look. 'Say
hello to the lady, Robert,' she instructed him in a thin
soft voice. 'Let her see you—come on now, show yourself.'

She seemed almost pushingly anxious to show him off,
but it was understandable in one way, for he was an
attractive child. About three years old, he had hair the
same sandy colour as his uncle's and his mother's, but
he had blue eyes instead of hazel as theirs were, and
he eyed her from the shelter of his mother's skirts—an

evasive, half-apprehensive survey that suggested he was unaccustomed to strangers.

'He's a lovely boy, Mrs——' Chiara paused awkwardly because she didn't remember the young woman having been given another name beside Betty.

'Betty,' Gavin answered for her. 'It's more friendly, is it not?'

'Oh yes, much more,' Chiara agreed. But she wondered why he was bothering to cover up when quite clearly his sister's fingers were devoid of a ring of any kind, a point she wished she had noticed sooner. Embarrassed both by her own gaffe and the attempted cover-up, she gave her attention to the child, smiling at his solemn face. 'How old are you, Robert?'

'He's three and two months,' his mother answered. 'He's bonny, is he not, with his big blue eyes? And he'll be tall too, taller than average, wouldn't you say, Miss Manti? A credit to any family.'

Chiara looked at the child rather than the mother because she found those narrow hazel eyes oddly discomfiting. As to whether or not the boy was likely to grow taller than average, she was no judge, and she admitted as much quite readily. 'I don't know how one tells at that age,' she confessed. 'But he's a fine big boy for three.'

It wasn't quite the reaction Betty McDonald had been looking for, judging by her expression, but she shrugged after a moment or two, and took the boy firmly by the hand again. 'If you'll excuse me for a wee while, Miss Manti, I'll take Robert to his bed. I'll not keep you long for your dinner.'

Gavin saw her seated in one of the big armchairs and seated himself facing her, but Chiara still found it hard to relax, although she could not understand why. When she looked at him and smiled, he gave her a small and faintly chill smile that did nothing to put her at ease, and clasped his hands together as he leaned forward in his chair.

'You'll have noticed,' he said, and it was a moment or two before Chiara realised that he referred to his sister's single status.

'That your sister isn't married?' she guessed, taking the bull by the horns. 'I'm sorry I—said what I did, I didn't do it deliberately, Gavin, I simply hadn't noticed.'

Gavin rested his elbows on his knees and didn't look at her. 'You're shocked?' he hazarded, and she shook her head very firmly.

'It's your business—yours and your sister's.'

'And the boy's father, surely!'

'And him too, of course,' she agreed quietly. She had a feeling it was all leading somewhere, but at the moment she couldn't see where, and she shook her head vaguely. 'I—I don't imagine your sister would like you talking to a stranger about it, Gavin.'

'It's something the whole village knows about!' Gavin claimed with such bitterness that it was obvious how much the scandal of his sister's behaviour had affected him. 'A bairn without a father, a woman without a man, and all because he——'

'Gavin, please!' It was something Chiara had no desire at all to become involved in, although she could understand and sympathise with his and his sister's bitterness. 'It isn't my business,' she pointed out gently, 'and I'd really much rather not discuss it. It—well, perhaps it wasn't the wisest thing for me to have come to your home in the circumstances, but I had no idea of the situation.'

'Or you'd not have come?' he guessed, and his eyes gleamed like topaz in the evening light. Then he heaved a sigh that Chiara had no doubt at all came from the heart, and shook his head slowly. 'It was perhaps unfair of me to try and involve you,' he allowed, 'but I thought——' He shrugged and spread his hands resignedly. 'I'm sorry, Chiara.'

'So am I,' she told him quietly, and ventured a faint smile. 'It seems a shame to spoil what could be a pleasant evening, so suppose we begin again, shall we?'

He nodded, but his sober gaze remained on her steadily for a moment so that she wondered what else he had in store for her, then he gave a slight shrug and seemed to recall that he was playing host. 'We've some sherry,' he said. 'Would you like some?'

'Yes, thank you, I would.'

Betty McDonald joined them very soon and from the way her strangely cold eyes darted from her brother to their visitor, Chiara suspected she knew she might have been the subject of their conversation. Then she noticed the faintest shake of Gavin's head and the way his sister caught her lower lip between her teeth and turned quickly to go into the kitchen. Something displeased her, Chiara thought, but she could not believe it was because Gavin had denied discussing her in her absence.

It promised to be a trying evening, and Chiara found no reason to change her opinion during the next couple of hours. Somehow she could not rid herself of the suspicion that she had been asked to the McDonald home for some purpose other than to be entertained to dinner, and the feeling was still with her when she left just after nine-thirty.

Gavin came out to the car with her and stood for a moment after he had seen her in and closed the car door. He was an attractive man and she liked him, but with her Latin love of life and laughter Chiara wished he was more animated, it would make so much difference. 'Will I see you again?' he asked, leaning down to speak to her through the car window, and Chiara smiled.

'If you'd like to,' she said.

'I'd like it fine!' he said unhesitatingly, and reached for her hand. The strength of his fingers surprised her, for they were short and slim and did not somehow seem like the hands of a farmer. 'We'll arrange something very soon.'

Seeing that he had nothing more definite in mind, Chiara started up the engine, leaving the window down because she had never yet ended a date without being kissed. But Gavin stepped back and waved a hand, calling goodnight as she drove off, and when she looked back by way of the rear-view mirror she saw him still standing there in the last of the evening light. A solitary and curiously lonely figure that somehow was rather touching; she was still thinking about him when she parked Campbell's car on the front drive and mounted the steps.

Campbell was in the hall when she started to open the door and he came across to help, for she always had difficulty with the huge iron-studded door. 'You're soon back,' he remarked as he closed it behind her. 'Did you not get along as well as you hoped with Gavin McDonald?'

'I got along very well with him,' she countered, more defiant than accurate. 'But farmers have to get up early!'

'So he cut short your evening,' said Campbell, shaking his head over what he saw as the other man's shortcomings. 'Och, he's no notion of romance, that man; he's as dour as a kirk elder!'

'He's very nice!' Chiara insisted, uncaring that the inevitable argument was looming if she went on. 'But— oh, I don't know.' She hesitated to say what she felt because she suspected Campbell might laugh at her. 'He's so very—serious, and his sister too; of course there is——'

She broke off when she realised how Campbell was looking at her. He no longer looked amused, but there was a tightness at the corners of his mouth that she had come to distrust, and he spoke in a low quiet voice that sent trickles along her spine. 'Are you telling me that he took you home to meet his sister?'

'Yes, and the little boy too.' She felt the same prickling sense of anticipation as when Gavin McDonald had broached the subject of his sister's unmarried state, and wondered exactly what deep waters ran beneath the seemingly placid life of the McDonalds. Raising her eyes, she looked at him directly, daring him to condemn the unfortunate Betty McDonald. 'I know all about Betty McDonald too,' she declared.

'Damn him!' Campbell thudded one huge fist on to a small table beside him, and Chiara stared at him, startled by his fierceness. 'Damn the pair of them for conniving to involve you!'

His harsh intolerance came as a shock, for it was not what she expected of him, and she shook her head urgently to deny it. 'Oh no, Campbell! How can you throw all the blame on to Betty McDonald? You couldn't be so—so unfair!'

He looked down at her with narrowed eyes, then gripped her arm suddenly and almost hauled her across the hall to a smaller sitting-room that was seldom used and struck damply chill as he closed the door behind them. He kept his hold on her while he switched on a table lamp, then pushed her down into a chair and stood towering over her, and she had never seen him look as he did then.

'So they told you that tale, did they?' he demanded. 'And you believed it all, of course—swallowed it hook, line and sinker—and relished the thought, no doubt!'

Completely at a loss, Chiara shook her head, looking up at him in wide-eyed bewilderment. The tip of her tongue moistened her lips, and Campbell gave a sigh of despair as he turned and walked across the room with one hand raking through his thick red-gold hair. Then he turned suddenly and she noticed the craggy lines that the dim lighting showed up on his face.

'That was why they asked you to the farm, of course! The McDonalds have never had visitors there since Betty came back there to live, but you had to get the full treatment—the whole sob-story with no doubt about who was the black-hearted villain who fathered that boy of hers!'

She stared at him in blank confusion for a moment. Even across the room she could feel the passion that burned in him, for there was nothing passive and docile about Campbell. He was a man who gave full rein to his passions and be damned to the consequences, and there was something about his concern over what the McDonalds might have told her that she found disturbing.

'Campbell, who is he? That little boy, who is he?'

His blue eyes burned fiercely and brightly in his strong dark face, and she noticed the arrogant way he held his head. 'Betty McDonald's son!' he stated harshly.

But something nagged at Chiara's brain relentlessly as she looked at him. She pondered on why Gavin McDonald, who hated Campbell, had invited her to his home after only one brief meeting, and why Betty McDonald had been so anxious to bring to her notice the fact that her child had blue eyes, and her insistence that he would grow to be taller than average—like the Roberts men.

Then the implication hit her like a sickening blow as she stared across the room, and Campbell came striding over to her, drawn by the realisation that was dawning in her eyes. 'It worked!' he said bitterly, and she flinched from the fierceness of his anger. 'You believe it; you believe that I fathered that bairn, I can see it in your eyes!'

'No!' The cry was dragged from her in a loud voice

that sounded nothing like hers at all. Then she swallowed hard when he scanned his vivid blue eyes over her face, and shook her head. 'If—if you tell me he isn't, then——'

'He isn't!' he declared firmly.

'Then——'

'It's what she decided to say,' he told her with a harsh burst of laughter. 'I believe several qualified for the honour, but eventually she decided I was the best prospect, being who I am, I suppose, only it didn't quite come off as she planned. I declined the privilege of marrying her!' A large and none too gentle hand was thrust under her chin and her head was jerked up so that she automatically looked up at him, meeting his eyes head on. 'Do you believe me?' he demanded.

Chiara moved her head, freeing herself from that disturbing contact, and quite convinced in her heart. 'I believe you because—you're not the type of man to duck your responsibilities, and you're much too arrogant to deny your own son whatever the circumstances!'

His bark of laughter made her jump, but it seemed to ease the tension of the past few minutes quite remarkably. 'Och, you're a bonny wee fighter!' he told her softly. 'Even when you're on my side you can't resist taking pot-shots at me, and I might have known Gavin McDonald couldn't get away with fooling you! You'll not be seeing him again?'

It was a statement rather than a question, and as such aroused her to a denial. 'I don't see why not!' she told him. 'He may well believe it's true, even if his sister knows it isn't.'

'But damn it, girl, he tried to put one over on you! Have you no family pride?'

Chiara got up from the chair he had pushed her into, and tried to keep a firm hold on her emotions, although it wasn't easy in the face of such arrogance, and she tilted her chin defiantly. 'Is it family pride that makes you so determined to marry me so that you can get your hands on whatever Grandpa leaves to me?' she asked.

The expression in his eyes was unfathomable as he lightly touched her cheek with a long forefinger and traced its curve down to her neck and the low edge of her dress. Then he slid a hand beneath her hair and pulled her close to him, burying his face in her hair so that his voice was low and muffled.

'Not entirely,' he whispered, and raised his head suddenly to swoop down on to her mouth. When he let her go she was breathless enough to cling to him and, holding her close, he rested his face on her hair, the warm vibrancy of him teasing her senses. 'I've seen you change through the years from a babe to a child,' he murmured, 'but the woman was more than I dared hope for. I've more than Castle Eyrie to gain now, I'll get myself a beautiful wife too.'

'No!' Chiara gathered the last remnants of her resistance and pulled away from him. She was shaking like a leaf as she looked up at him with black reproachful eyes, and she slipped quickly out of his arms while he was unprepared for it, to go hurrying across the little room. But when she turned to close the door she noticed that he was smiling again, and there was something about that smile that disturbed her. 'No!' she declared firmly to herself as she crossed the hall.

'No, no, no—I *won't*!'

CHAPTER FOUR

It was a day or two before Chiara heard any more about Campbell's invitation to dine out with him. In fact she had begun to think that either he had forgotten about it or he had never intended it seriously in the first place, when he suddenly announced that they were driving into Kerside that same evening, and the question of whether or not she was prepared to go seemed not to enter into it.

Kerside was the only town of any size that was near enough and likely to have a restaurant able to provide dinner, and it did not even occur to Chiara to object to his high-handed arrangements; it was something that she now took for granted as part of his character. In fact she looked forward to seeing him in different surroundings, and judging him in what she privately termed a more civilised setting.

A dark suit worn with a white shirt and a tie laid a veneer of sophistication on that more familiar earthiness, but he would always be an eye-catching man, whatever the circumstances, and she found him attractive however firmly she refused to consider marrying him. He seemed to have acquired a slightly more polished manner along with his change of dress and environment too, although a disturbing glint of speculation still lurked in his eyes whenever he looked at her.

They were at the coffee stage of their meal when Chiara caught sight of someone on the other side of the restaurant obviously trying to catch his eye, and she drew his attention to the fact. Campbell turned and smiled, acknowledging recognition with a casual wave of a hand, and when he turned back to her, Chiara could not resist a question.

'A friend of yours?' she enquired, and he regarded her quizzically for a moment.

'You could say so.'

Chiara held her coffee cup in both hands and studied its contents while she spoke. 'I notice she has red hair.'

'So?' he prompted.

She shrugged. 'So you told me that your taste always runs to redheads; I was just confirming it, that's all.'

'Not always,' Campbell argued, his eyes gleaming. 'You're living proof of that, surely.'

'Oh, Cam!' She had never before used the abbreviation of his name, and judging by his expression he didn't like it much. 'I'm a means to an end, not a deviation from your taste for redheads, and I don't fool myself it's any more than that.'

'You're fooling yourself if you believe that's all you are,' he informed her with a half-smile, and the look in those heavy-lidded blue eyes did alarming things to her pulse for a moment. 'I may have called you a black-eyed brat the last time you were here,' he went on, 'but you're a black-eyed beauty now and I'm not too set on redheads that I can't be converted.'

'You'd do anything to get your hands on the whole of Grandpa's estate,' Chiara declared crossly, 'and I know it, that's what gives me an advantage. Warning me was a mistake from your point of view, because if you hadn't told me what you had in mind, I——'

She stopped there, realising suddenly the reason for the glinting laughter in his eyes, and the colour flooded into her face as she hastily reached for her wine glass to cover her confusion. 'If I hadn't told you what I had in mind,' he went on for her, in that soft and dangerously persuasive voice, 'you might have been a willing partner, is that what you were going to say, Chiara?'

'I was going to say,' Chiara told him swiftly, 'that I might have been easier to persuade if you hadn't shown me what a mercenary, heartless and unfeeling monster you are!'

It was debatable which of them realised first that she did not mean a word of it, and when he reached across and touched the back of her hand lightly with his fingers she didn't draw back, nor was she able to do anything about the thudding beat of her heart that the deliberately seductive caress aroused.

'I *have* enjoyed this evening,' she allowed huskily, 'but I would have enjoyed it more if I hadn't known your motive for bringing me.'

'You're a very lovely and a very sexy little female,' Campbell said softly, 'that was my motive for bringing you. If you think otherwise you're doing both yourself and me an injustice, Chiara.'

She wanted so much to believe him and the fact influenced her response whether or not she realised it. She had enjoyed her evening and not least she had enjoyed his company; the Italian atmosphere, the food and even speaking for a few moments to the wine waiter in the more familiar Italian, had given her pleasure, she couldn't deny it.

'It was nice of you to bring me to an Italian restaurant,' she said eventually, and Campbell gave her a curiously lopsided kind of smile.

'I do try to please you occasionally,' he claimed. 'I thought you might be feeling a wee bit homesick, and the sight and sound of a few familiar things might be welcome.'

'It was very thoughtful of you—thank you.'

'I'm glad you enjoyed it.' A smile lingered in the vivid blue eyes that regarded her across the table. 'Now mebbe you'll come with me again some time.'

Chiara didn't commit herself, but a half-smile suggested her willingness, if he should ask again. The bill was paid and the waiter generously tipped, if his expression was an indication, and they got up to leave. But even while he solicitously guided her between the tables with a hand under her arm, Campbell turned and waved a farewell hand at the redhaired woman.

Chiara's frown was instinctive, and when he caught her eye he half-smiled and raised a brow in query. 'You don't mind, do you?' he asked.

It rather surprised Chiara to realise that in fact she did mind, but she would have died rather than let him know it, and she shrugged carelessly. 'Of course I don't mind, why should I?'

'Why should you?' Campbell echoed, and she coloured warmly at the brief sound of his laughter.

As they drove home the countryside was bathed in moonlight, and the tree-dark slopes of the hills had an air of mystery that reminded her of the books she had so avidly read ever since her schooldays. Romantic adventures set in the violent and stirring times of Scotland's history and peopled with men like the one who sat beside her now. Half-turning her head, she realised just how perfectly Campbell fitted into the role of those fictional heroes, and the recognition of it affected her strangely.

Moonlight added deeper lines and shadows to his craggy features, and there was a brooding, sometimes almost savage look about him that stirred her own blood alarmingly. He was hers if she chose to accept him, and she had little doubt that had he not been so frank about his reason for wanting to marry her she would have happily taken him for a husband and loved him as passionately as even he could desire.

But she caught herself up suddenly when she realised the depth and direction of her own ramblings, and very deliberately she turned her mind to a side of him that could help to keep her as firmly resolved against marrying him. 'Just how many redheads have you—do you know, Campbell?'

Obviously she had startled him, for he turned his head swiftly and frowned. 'Now what are you getting at?' he demanded.

Chiara shrugged, keeping her eyes on the steep, winding moonlit road. 'I just wondered if you have a reputation as a—a——'

His laughter cut short her groping uncertainty, and she looked at him uneasily from the corner of her eye. 'You want to know if I'm as friendly with the local lassies as our notorious ancestor was, is that it?'

'Our—I don't know anything about a notorious ancestor.'

'You don't?' He was smiling as if he relished telling her the tale whatever it was. 'I'm surprised your mother didn't tell you about him. John Roberts—he was alive around the end of the eighteenth century and he was quite a lad, according to local legend. He's certainly responsible for the fact that the Lussie lads are quite often look-alikes for our family, and he played such havoc with our family reputation that his father shipped him off to the States where, presumably, he died, for he was never heard of again.'

'I see.'

Her response, she thought, disappointed him a little, although she did not question the validity of the story, and he gave her a swift and speculative glance sideways. 'Och, Chiara,' he said softly, 'you take it all so seriously! If you're working round to giving me a reputation lurid as John Roberts' you'll be doing me an injustice, I promise you. Oh, I'm not a saint by any means, I don't claim to be; I'm nearly thirty-four years old and I like the lassies, and they, bless their hearts, seem to like me. With exceptions, of course,' he added with a half-smile. 'But I've never been responsible for unwanted bairns all over the landscape, and I've never broken any hearts yet, and that includes Betty McDonald's.'

His reply was oddly chastening. Although she had not consciously been thinking about Gavin McDonald's sister, Chiara supposed it had been in the back of her mind, and there was no escaping the fact that she too was a redhead, even if a sandy one. Keeping her eyes determinedly on the thickly forested slopes of Castle Eyrie, she tried to correct the impression she might have given.

'I've already told you that I take your word for that,' she reminded him in a slightly reproachful voice. 'Seeing that woman in the restaurant and remembering what you'd said about preferring redheads, I just wondered, that's all.'

'You wouldn't be just a wee bit jealous, would you?' he suggested in that stunningly soft accent, and Chiara shook her head firmly. 'Oh well——' he sighed, and she did not for a moment believe he was as disappointed as he sounded.

Distracted for a moment by the familiarity of the thickly wooded hillside, Chiara could imagine it as alive with all the creatures that Campbell set such store by. It gave her a brief thrill of momentary fear to remember that somewhere behind an invisible steel fence those sleek grey wolves padded silently through the moonlit forest as they had done hundreds of years ago, and she started visibly when a sudden long-drawn-out howl wailed through the still night air, sounding much too close for comfort.

'Old Lonesome baying at the moon,' Campbell speculated, and his smile told her that he had noted her flinch at the sound. 'Noisy old devil, he'll be bringing me complaints if he makes a habit of it.'

'That big rather scuffy-looking one with the awful eyes?' Chiara asked, then shivered again when the animal once more gave vent to his solitary complaint.

'That's him,' Campbell agreed. 'He's never run with the rest of the pack and we've never been able to make out why. What the——!' He cursed under his breath and slowed the car almost to a standstill while he peered through the windscreen at something, although when Chiara looked she saw nothing but the shadows of the trees.

Her heart was thudding hard, though she had no notion why, except that the howl of the wolf had brought a nerve-tingling air of expectancy in its wake. 'What is it?' she asked, and Campbell gave a brief snort of amusement.

'Courting couple, most likely,' he said. 'I damn near ran into somebody. First they dived into the trees and then changed direction and went scuttling down the bank on the other side of the road. Whoever it was probably recognised the car and thought better of doing his courting on our land.' He kept the car at a crawling pace, and there was obviously something on his mind. 'Funny,' he mused, 'I swear I saw only one of them.'

'A poacher?' Chiara suggested, but he shook his head.

'Not likely; there's easier pickings in the wood by Roberts' Brae. Much better for the kind of game you're talking about.' He drew the car over to the side of the road and switched off the engine. 'I'll take the flashlight and have a look around,' he said, reaching into the glove compartment. 'I'm not a spoilsport, but I'd rather the wildlife was kept to the four-legged kind.'

It was uncannily still once the engine was switched off, and when he got out of the car Chiara did too. 'I'm not staying here on my own,' she told him in response to a raised brow. 'I'll come with you.'

'In those shoes?' He directed the torch on to her feet in dainty blue shoes, and she realised how awkward it would be walking in them over rough ground. 'You stay in the car,' he said persuasively. 'I'll not be more than a minute or two, and you'll be O.K.; if you're nervous lock the door after me.'

He saw her back into the car, giving her no opportunity to argue the point, then went striding off into the black mystery of the forest. The comforting eye of the flashlight disappeared with dismaying swiftness and even with the windows closed she could hear the faint sounds that rustled softly among the trees, suggesting constant movement and a sense of being watched. When after several moments the chilling wail of the wolf howled mournfully at the moon, she shivered, and safer or not she got out of the car and pulled the collar of her light coat more closely around her throat.

There was no glimmer of torchlight anywhere, and no sound of Campbell; he must be as soft-footed as his precious wolves. But as she moved further into the trees she was confronted by small yellow dots that glimmered in the moonlight and watched with baleful steadiness. A series of sounds, like dogs snuffling, and the yellow eyes were gone, leaving her skin chill and prickling with goose-pimples.

'Campbell?' Her voice shivered uncertainly, but there was no reply, only small mysterious sounds that she couldn't identify. 'Campbell, where are you?'

She slipped when she caught her foot on a tree root and almost went down, and her gasp of dismay sounded incredibly loud in the stillness. Her scalp crawled with the sensation of being observed, and she darted anxious glances around the concealing trees, reminding herself that she had been there dozens of times in daylight; it was familiar ground.

She was just about managing to stave off a sense of panic when she heard the distinct sound of a stick snapping, as if someone had trodden on it, and she turned swiftly, trying to see through the tangle of shadows made by the trees. More than likely it was Campbell, but there was the possibility that there was someone else about and she stood with her hands holding the coat tightly about her throat and scarcely daring to breathe.

The moment he stepped into view and she saw the gleam of red-gold hair she heaved such a massive sigh of relief that he found her at once. 'I might have known you'd not do as you were told,' he remarked without rancour, and stood facing her, looking down into her face with shadow-darkened eyes for a moment. 'Moonlight becomes you,' he crooned quietly, then bent and lightly kissed her mouth. 'Come away home, girl, there's nobody here who shouldn't be.'

He had barely finished speaking when the solitary wolf again bayed his loneliness to the moon, and Chiara started nervously catching her breath and clutching involuntarily at Campbell's arm. She looked over at the wolf compound and her fingers tightened when she caught sight of dark shapes slinking away.

Turning her to face him, Campbell took both her arms, looking down at her for a moment, his strong fingers reassuringly firm. 'You're as nervous as a wee kitten,' he teased gently. 'Old Lonesome'll not hurt you, he's safely behind bars, and I'm here with you, now what could hurt you, eh?'

'Nothing, I suppose,' Chiara admitted, 'but it's—it's spooky, and you were gone such a long time.'

'A few minutes, that's all,' he assured her softly. 'Mebbe it seemed longer, eh?'

Chiara made no reply and it was inevitable, she felt, when he drew her into his arms. She went without hesitation and allowed herself to lean against the long, lean reassuring length of him; and resting her head against his chest she could feel the thudding beat of his heart. Her own, she knew, beat even faster than his when he bent his head and pressed his lips to the warm skin of her neck.

His hands slid around her, pressing her closer, and his mouth touched her ear, nibbling gently at the lobe until she raised her head and exposed the soft vulnerability of her throat. Her eyelids fluttered, half-closed and making smudged shadows on her cheeks while he lightly kissed her throat and jaw, and the curve of her cheek, until he found what he was seeking in the warm eager softness of her mouth.

Just as it had been the wolf's baying that brought her into his arms, the same sound brought her back to awareness and she made a small murmur of sound as she freed her mouth, then put both hands to his chest to hold him at bay. Her heart was beating wildly and her legs felt too unsteady to support her, nevertheless she broke his hold and stepped back from him, thanking heaven that the moonlight disguised the flush that warmed her cheeks.

'It's time we went home,' she whispered huskily, and Campbell said nothing for a moment. Then he nodded, and it somehow surprised her that he neither smiled nor mocked her for bringing the moment to an end, but took her arm and guided her through the trees back to the car. He saw her into her seat, then came round and slid behind the wheel, glancing briefly back the way they had come before he started the engine.

'Whoever it was has gone,' he assured her. 'Mebbe there were two of them went down the bank after all; it's hard to tell in the moonlight.' Chiara was still coping with her uncertain emotions and when she didn't answer he turned and looked at her briefly. 'I'll not say I'm sorry, Chiara,' he told her quietly, and he seemed so much more serious than ever he had before. 'But I don't think you want me to, do you?'

'No.' She whispered the denial, and he reached and covered her hands with one of his own. 'I—I don't think you have to, Campbell; you've kissed me before.'

'Aye, I have.' He was still so much more sober than usual, and she wondered what had made this particular instance so different from the other times. His strong fingers grasped hers tightly for a moment, then he once more put both hands on the wheel, but Chiara had the feeling that he too had felt something different about this occasion. 'I have,' he echoed, almost as if he spoke to himself.

Campbell was off quite early the following morning, on horseback, and Chiara took the Land Rover down to the compound to see what she could do. Most often her help was needed to drive to the suppliers for feedstuffs, or else to put out the food for the creatures whose continued survival depended on it, and she had so far managed to drive without further mishap.

Murdoch, Campbell's helper, had taken quite a fancy to her now that he knew her better, and although he was a dour and largely uncommunicative man on the whole, he was doing more to convert her to the cause of conservation than anyone. In fact she felt that it was Murdoch rather than Campbell to whom she was most help.

She had left the Land Rover with Murdoch and continued on foot, and was watching a pine marten whisking back and forth along a pine branch when she became aware of another kind of activity some distance away. Where she stood she was concealed in a brake of young larch, but the figure that stooped down beside the steel mesh of the wolf enclosure was in full view, and it was neither of the men who had a right to be there.

Crouched over and busy with something low down near the ground, it was hard to identify as either male or female, and trousers and a baggy sweater with a woollen hat pulled right over the hair made it even harder to tell. Whoever it was, Chiara felt they had no business there, and when she recalled how Campbell had almost run someone down last night she was even more suspicious.

It was purely on impulse that she acted as she did; stepping into view at the fringe of the larch trees she called out, 'Hey!'

The crouching figure straightened at once, scrambling clumsily in its haste, then started running without a backward glance, going fast and weaving in and out of the trees, sure-footed as a deer and soon out of sight. It would be little use following, she thought, but she would have made an attempt if something had not caught her eye suddenly.

Right at the bottom of the mesh fence was a break, a deliberate cut several inches high and with the corners turned outward to make a hole; small, but ample to allow an animal to slip out to freedom. She caught her breath and stepped back into the shelter of the trees again, when she noticed something even more alarming.

A hand to her mouth to stifle any further involuntary sounds, she watched the creature who came padding swiftly along the perimeter of the compound. Old Lonesome, Campbell had christened him, with his penchant for naming the beasts he treasured so much, and at the moment Chiara could only thank heaven that it was the solitary animal and not the whole pack.

Gnawing anxiously at her lip, she tried to summon courage enough to drive the animal back, but no matter how often Campbell assured her that the wolves were unlikely to harm anyone, she simply could not bring herself to step out of concealment and face it alone. By now the long nose was sniffing out a way of escape, and she stood as if frozen, with a hand covering her mouth.

The wolf slid down on to its lean belly and eased its length through the damaged mesh, flattening its thick grey fur to accommodate the small opening. Once free it lifted its muzzle for a second and sniffed the air, then, head down, it loped off through the trees to freedom. Not until it was safely out of sight did Chiara dare to venture near the cut fence, and she blamed herself for being such a coward as she took off the scarf she wore at the neck of her shirt and used it to make a hasty repair.

She had never run so fast in her life before as when she went in search of Murdoch, and she was breathing hard when she came on him at the far end, talking to Campbell. Campbell noticed how distressed she was and came hurrying over to her, his eyes anxious. 'Chiara, what on earth's the matter?'

'One of the wolves,' she panted breathlessly, and saw the way his mouth tightened suddenly. 'It's out and away!'

'How?' he demanded shortly, but he was already mounting the big grey stallion he always rode, and Chiara answered him as briefly.

'Someone cut a hole in the fence; I've stopped it temporarily. It's old Lonesome, Campbell.'

'Damn!' He swore furiously, but he was already organising something more practical too. 'Murdoch, drive Miss Manti up to the house and get yourself a horse, then follow after me; we'll need to go on four legs to catch up with that crafty old devil. And you stay in the house, Chiara, out of harm's way!'

She was already in the Land Rover before he finished speaking, and Murdoch drove like a wild man up the steep hill to the castle, then left her at the door while he went to saddle himself a horse. It would be useless to try and follow an animal like the wolf in a motor vehicle, and for the first time in her life Chiara wished she had learned to ride.

She went and found her grandfather in his own sitting-room and was amazed when he mourned his inability to join the hunt. 'Time was,' he complained bitterly, 'when I'd have given that young limmer a run for his money, now——' He shrugged his broad stooping shoulders resignedly. 'Och, why does a man have to grow old, Chiara?'

'It happens to everybody,' Chiara consoled him, but found it hard to imagine it ever happening to Campbell, who was so much like him.

That hard, virile body seemed destined to survive for ever as it was, anything else did not bear thinking about, and yet Ian Roberts had once looked exactly as Campbell did now—photographs showed that. Recognising the inevitability of it brought little shivers of ice along Chiara's spine and she turned once more to look out of the window.

The old man's room looked out over the miles of rolling moorland that stretched on seemingly endlessly below the sheer drop that isolated Castle Eyrie on its pinnacle of grandeur. She could see the crags where the golden eagle nested, and where wildcats lurked among the rock crevices; and the heather where grouse and hares made ready prey for the predators.

Over to her left was where Gavin McDonald grazed his sheep, and as she watched, extending her vision to the limit, something nearer home and in the foreground caught her eye—a low, loping form that looked like a large dog from her vantage point was making for those smoother, more nourishing pastures where the sheep grazed.

'Grandpa!' She turned quickly and caught her grandfather's frown. 'I've spotted it! That wretched wolf, it's making for Gavin McDonald's sheep, and if anything happens——' She hurried across the room, pausing only briefly when the old man called out to her.

'Where are you going, girl? Take care!'

'I have to warn Gavin,' she told him, and was already

half-way out of the door. 'I'll take the Land Rover and drive round to the farm; he might be able to do something. I have to warn him!'

'Chiara!'

She went on, unheeding, and dashed downstairs. She didn't bother telling her aunt where she was going, for Margaret Roberts would not encourage such an errand, but went straight on through the hall and out to the Land Rover that still stood by the front door. As she drove it down the track to the road, she wondered what Campbell's reaction would be, but in the circumstances hoped he would agree she was doing the right thing.

Thanking heaven that she had not to drive as far as the village, she drove at top speed down the approach to the McDonalds' farm and then remembered that the front door was never used. It was obvious that she was the very last person that Gavin expected to see driving furiously into his yard, and he stared for a moment before coming across to her.

'Gavin,' she called, even before she got out of the vehicle, 'thank goodness you're here! One of the wolves is out and making for your sheep—I thought you might be able to——'

He cut her short by swearing virulently, and his hazel eyes burned fiercely as he went striding into the house without a backward glance. Chiara was still standing, rather dazedly, by the Land Rover when he came out again, and she caught her lip anxiously between her teeth when she noted that he was armed with a sporting gun.

It hadn't occurred to her until then that Campbell and Murdoch may have hoped to capture the animal before it could do any damage, but if Gavin McDonald spotted old Lonesome he would shoot without hesitation and, she suspected, be glad of the excuse to make his point about Campbell's security arrangements.

'Stay indoors, and keep the laddie with you!' Gavin

shouted the warning over his shoulder, and Chiara caught only a glimpse of Betty McDonald's thin face and sandy hair before she closed the door. His eyes narrow and angry, Gavin spared her only a minute, and Chiara shrank from the look on his face.

'So much for your assurance that those beasts were securely fenced!' he said coldly, and got quickly into a battered jeep that stood in the yard. 'You'd best get home!'

'But, Gavin, someone——'

'I've no time,' he snapped bitterly, 'I've my flock to look to!'

It was no use trying to tell him that the fence had been cut deliberately, she realised. Even if he had the time to stop and listen it would to some extent exonerate Campbell from blame, and Gavin, she realised, wouldn't want to do that. She gave a last look at the firmly closed door of the farmhouse, then got back into the Land Rover.

It was too easy to just go home and do nothing, and Chiara drove on the road for only a short distance after she left the farm, then turned off suddenly, her mind made up to go and find Campbell if she could. Another pair of eyes might well be useful, and she had after all already made one sighting.

Unthinking about whether or not she might actually hinder the search, she drove across the jolting tussocks of heather as fast as she dared, and she had gone some distance from the road when she spotted Campbell and Murdoch over near a line of crags. She spun the wheel quickly to change direction, and the vehicle swung sharply, then came to a sudden jerking halt and stopped dead.

The silence, as it always did, seemed to flow around her, and she sat for a second or two helplessly wondering what had happened. She was completely without knowledge of even basic mechanics, but when she took a look at the various dials on the dashboard it didn't need mechanical knowledge to know that no vehicle goes very far without petrol, and she heaved a great sigh of exasperation as she climbed out.

She frowned for a moment, then pinpointed the two men she sought at the foot of the crags, and circling slowly around the group of rocks as if they sought a means of access to the heights. Just over to their left and with a narrow burn between them, Gavin McDonald stopped the jeep he was driving and got out, then reached into the back of it for something, and raised the gun to his shoulder.

She saw the sun glinting on the long barrel and started to run; she wasn't quite sure what she hoped to do, but apparently his target had vanished again, for he lowered the gun and stood with it under his arm; a patient, menacing figure in the peaceful setting. It was Campbell who spotted her coming, almost inevitably, and he came riding over, jabbing the grey angrily with his heels.

'What the devil are you doing out here?' he demanded, and Chiara fought for breath enough to tell him.

She pointed across the burn. 'I—went to warn—Gavin McDonald, then—then I realised——'

'Damn you, Chiara!' He gave one hard fierce glance across the tiny stream that separated him from his neighbour, then turned his anger back on her. 'You've got the fool out gunning for him, and it wasn't necessary!'

'I'm sorry.' His fury hurt, and she thought it ought to have made her angry instead, but there wasn't time to analyse her emotions at the moment. 'I—I thought about the sheep; I saw the wolf coming this way and——'

'You went running to tell him so that he could go on the rampage!' Campbell rasped harshly, looking down at her from the stallion's back. 'This was all he needed— an excuse to prove that I'm endangering his livelihood by keeping the animals, don't you see that?'

'I—I didn't think.'

Her lip trembled, but either he didn't notice or he
didn't care as he once more looked across at Gavin's
still and patient figure waiting for his enemy to appear so
that he could destroy him. 'We've a net and we hope to
be able to catch him,' Campbell's voice broke into her
misery. 'The creature knows Murdoch and there's a
chance he'll respond if we can get close enough.' He
glanced over his shoulder at the shorter figure of Murdoch, on foot and hefting a thick black net in his hands.
'I'm needed,' he told her abruptly. 'Go home, Chiara, and
for the love of God stay out of mischief!'

He turned before she had time to reply, and Chiara
watched him rejoin Murdoch, then together they began
a slow and careful climb up the face of the crags. What
happened next happened so quickly that she was almost
unaware of the significance of it. Campbell and Murdoch
were about half way up the steep incline when the wolf
suddenly appeared right at the very pinnacle of the crags
and just for a moment stood silhouetted against the skyline.

It was the chance that Gavin McDonald had been waiting for, and he raised his gun to his shoulder again.
Campbell's cry came too late or was unheeded, and the
shot rang out, flattened and softened by distance and the
open air, and a bloodcurdling yelp was followed by utter
and complete silence. The silhouette no longer showed
on the skyline and tears rolled down Chiara's cheeks un-
checked when she saw Campbell beat his clenched fists
on the bare rock before burying his head against his fore-
arms in despair.

She was still sitting where he had left her when Campbell came and found her shortly afterwards, and his feelings were plain on his face. His vivid blue eyes burned
fiercely, and the lines at the corners of his mouth were

much more sharply etched than they normally were, so that something in her wanted to reach out to him with comfort.

'He's dead.' He might have been talking about the death of a friend and in a way Chiara felt the effect must have been much the same, for he had a close affinity with the wild creatures he fought so hard to re-establish in their original habitat.

'I'm sorry, I really am.'

A hand brushed tears from her cheeks, but he seemed unmoved, or perhaps he suspected her of having a motive for producing tears. 'You surely didn't walk all this way, did you?' he demanded next, and she shook her head.

'I—I had the Land Rover, but it ran out of petrol.'

'Not surprising when you go careering about all over the countryside in it!' he declared flatly, and Chiara looked up at him with a spark of the old defiance in her eyes.

'I did what I thought was right,' she told him. 'And you don't have to take it out on me, Campbell! Gavin was within his rights to shoot if he thought his flock was in danger!'

His eyes blazed down at her, and even the stallion seemed to sense the fury in him, for it shifted restlessly, only to be brought round with a sharp pull on the bit. 'Then let him drive you home!' he told her, and put his heels to the horse, sending him racing off to where Murdoch was waiting patiently for him.

He should have known, Chiara told herself, that Gavin wouldn't realise she needed a lift home, and she was both angry and hurt as she turned and started to walk the long way back to the road. The jeep was already long gone and no doubt Gavin was almost home, well pleased to have proved his point. At the moment Chiara hated both him and Campbell with equal fury because both saw only their own points of view and she had landed somewhere in the middle.

She hadn't gone very far before she heard something behind her that made her turn about quickly, recognising the sound of hooves only when she saw the stallion bearing down on her and Campbell tall and tight-lipped in the saddle. Trembling and with her eyes half concealed by lowered lids, she stood and waited for him, and something in her heart leapt at the possibility of his having had a change of heart.

He stopped right beside her so that she cast a wary eye at the huge animal's tossing head. 'Give me your hand!' Campbell ordered, and thrust his own big one down for her to take.

'But——'

It was fear of his mount that made her hesitate, but he was in no mood for prevaricating, whatever her reason, and he leaned down and glared into her face. 'Give me your hand and put your foot in the stirrup,' he repeated sharply, 'and for God's sake don't take all day about it!'

Obediently she grasped the hand he proffered and put her foot in the empty stirrup iron as he said, then she gave a small squeak of alarm as she was hauled swiftly upward and landed without ceremony pillion-fashion behind him. She needed no advice to hold on tightly, and there was something undeniably pleasurable about placing both arms around him and hugging close to the familiar and reassuring solidity of his body.

The sensation of riding, even as she did, was not at all as she anticipated, and there was something thrilling about galloping along with the wind whipping her hair back from her face, and the thudding of the horse's hooves like a drumbeat that pounded through her whole body as the stallion made its surefooted way back to Castle Eyrie.

They were approaching the steep incline that led to

the rear of the castle before she spoke, and her voice had a light and faintly husky sound as she spoke close to the broad expanse of his shoulder. 'I've often thought I'd like to ride,' she ventured, and Campbell half-turned his head as if the response was more automatic than voluntary.

'You'd better learn,' he said shortly. 'Then I shan't be required to come and rescue you every time you get yourself stranded!'

It wasn't exactly a gallant response, Chiara thought as she slid her arms a little further around him, but at least he had come back for her, and she found it hard to believe that it pleased her so much.

CHAPTER FIVE

It had not occurred to Chiara that her uncle could be in ignorance of his son's plan to marry her, yet it seemed he was. Nothing very much happened on Sundays, although Campbell still needed to see that the animals were fed, and Chiara was taking a stroll in the garden with her uncle while Aunt Margaret checked on the final stages of the meal. Chiara had been expressing her regret at what had happened the day before, and made no attempt to disguise the fact that her regret was primarily because of the effect on Campbell.

'Oh, but he understands why you did what you did, my dear,' Colin assured her. 'Don't worry about it.'

Recalling how angry Campbell had been, and how much less communicative he had seemed since, Chiara doubted it, and she pulled a rueful face. 'Oh well, at least it might prove to him that I'm not the ideal wife for such a firm conservationist as he is,' she said, and noticed the way he reacted.

He regarded her with slightly narrowed eyes and his smile suggested that he wasn't sure whether to take her seriously. 'Did the question of you being suitable ever arise, my dear? I didn't know. Not,' he hastened to add, 'that I have any objection at all, and your relationship isn't as close as first cousins would normally be, of course, with Marie and me being only half-brother and sister, but I'd no idea things were so—advanced between you.'

'Oh, they're not, except in Campbell's estimation,' Chiara assured him. She was already regretting the impulse that had led to her making such a rash observation, but it was too late now to draw back. 'He informed me that he was going to marry me, about the second or third day I was here; the idea being, of course, that he could then get control of *all* Grandpa Roberts' estate instead of just half of it.'

'Oh, my dear child, I had no idea!' It would be exaggerating to say that he looked shocked, but clearly he was stunned by his son's mercenary outlook and did not quite understand her apparently matter-of-fact view of it. 'But why didn't you tell me about this before, Chiara? You're very young to cope with something like that, and I can only think that Cam must have been out of his head when he made such a suggestion with so little—finesse and so soon.'

'On the contrary,' Chiara denied with a rather cynical little smile, 'it's a very practical solution, looked at from his point of view!'

Her uncle frowned, and it was clear he didn't quite know what to make of the situation. 'But to behave so thoughtlessly towards you! No wonder he didn't say anything to me about it!'

A certain tone in his voice warned her that he might well tackle Campbell with it the next time he saw him, and Chiara hastened to forestall the idea. Campbell and his father disagreeing over her was something she could well do without, and it would simply give Aunt Margaret further cause to see her as a disruptive influence.

'Oh, I can cope with Campbell,' she assured him with more conviction than she felt. 'He knows how I feel, and I think he knows that I mean it when I say I wouldn't marry him if he was the last man on earth!'

'So adamant, my dear? Wouldn't you even consider marrying him in any circumstances?'

For a moment Chiara wondered if, on reflection, he appreciated the advantages from his son's point of view. And she couldn't truthfully say that she wouldn't ever consider marrying him because more and more lately she found herself only too ready to be influenced by Campbell's vigorous brand of sex-appeal, so that the situation was fraught with threats to her determined resistance.

Nevertheless she didn't want to risk even a suggestion that she was weakening, to get back to him, and she shook her head firmly. 'Campbell knows I've no intention of letting myself be persuaded by his—as he sees it—right to Castle Eyrie,' she told him. 'When I marry, whoever it is, I shall marry for love, Uncle Colin, just as my mother did.'

'And isn't it possible you could do that and still marry Cam?' her uncle suggested quietly.

It was, Chiara realised, only too possible, but caution still guarded her tongue. 'I can't see it at the moment,' she said. 'He's too determined to get his own way, and I don't much like being told that I'm merely—useful to him.' She gave him a brief and slightly rueful smile. 'I imagine Campbell doesn't have much trouble getting his own way with women as a rule, and he's still trying to work out why I don't give in gracefully.'

They strolled on in silence along red gravel paths between borders of shrubs, and Chiara got the impression that her uncle was trying to make up his mind about something. It was several moments before she learned what was on his mind, and clearly he was still undecided about the wisdom of mentioning it. 'You'll know about the business of Betty McDonald?' he ventured, and immediately Chiara's heart began a hard urgent beat.

'I know she has a child, and that she *hasn't* a husband,' she agreed, then pressed on before he could comment. 'I also know that Campbell isn't the baby's father because Campbell told me he isn't, and whatever else he is he's honest—brutally so sometimes!'

'Ah, that'll not be why you won't marry him, then?'

'No, of course not!' she denied firmly.

'There's someone else, maybe?' her uncle queried, and it was clear that he was now looking for reasons himself why she did not accept his son's proposal. 'A boy-friend perhaps in Italy?'

Chiara shook her head. 'No, there's no one; no one serious, that is.' She thought she knew what he was leading up to and it was hard to believe that nice kind Uncle Colin was actually trying to persuade her towards marrying Campbell, even if his motives were purely mercenary. 'Uncle Colin, you surely don't expect me to marry Campbell in—in cold blood, do you? I can't believe you mean it!'

His eyes showed a glimmer of mischief for a moment and he shook his head slowly. 'Och, you'd not find him cold-blooded, girl,' he promised, 'and you'd make a handsome pair, the two of you. There's never been a black-eyed Roberts before!'

'Uncle Colin!'

'Ah, now don't judge too hastily, child,' he scolded gently. 'You could do much worse; he's a good man for all he's a roving eye for the lassies, and I guarantee he'd not stray after he was married to you!'

'No!' She protested as much from habit as because she believed he meant it all seriously, and when she saw the way he was smiling, she wondered why she had never realised before how much of a tease he was, for all his kindness. Campbell was very much like him except that he had the bolder and more aggressive manner of their grandfather. 'I couldn't marry anyone in those kind of circumstances,' she insisted, 'and least of all Campbell!'

His kindly eyes showed regret when he regarded her for a moment. 'You like him, do you not?' he asked, as if he could not believe otherwise, and Chiara did not look at him.

Her heart beat hard and fast when she only thought about the way Campbell had kissed her that night—

the urgent mouth seeking hers, so much more gentle than ever before yet so wantonly seductive that her whole being had responded to the touch of him. A dangerous reaction when all he wanted was her share of Castle Eyrie.

'I like him well enough,' she replied, studiously under-stating, 'but I won't marry him, Uncle Colin. I'm sorry if you feel I'm being too finicky, but it just isn't the way I've been brought up. This isn't the Middle Ages, and people don't marry for those kind of reasons any more.'

She didn't stop to think that his own wife had married him for reasons very similar, and it was too late by the time she realised. But at least he loved Aunt Margaret for all her faults, and Chiara had yet to be convinced that Campbell saw her as anything more than a means to an end who also happened to be a pretty girl.

'Ah well,' Colin said cheerfully as they turned back towards the house, 'it's early days yet!'

It was sheer restlessness that sent Chiara out walking over the moors after lunch, for she always felt very much an intruder still whenever she spent any length of time in her aunt's company. Campbell was off out again immediately after lunch, riding, presumably, since he had been wearing the cords and half-boots that he customarily wore on horseback.

Walking wasn't something she had often indulged in, although her mother had claimed to be a tireless walker in her youth, and must often have come the same way that Chiara came now. There was a kind of peace to be found out there that she had never found elsewhere, and she was beginning to realise how it was that her mother had still sometimes been homesick even after twenty years away.

It was vast and rugged and beautiful, and it had a feeling of agelessness that was at once stirring and tranquil, like being at the edge of the world. The soft blues and greens smoothed and gentled the harshness of mountains and crags, while the loch lay like a huge dark mirror that reflected only the broad lift of the sky.

She might be lucky and catch sight of old Yellow Nose, she thought, and with that in mind she made her way towards the loch and the eagle's habitual hunting grounds. It occurred to her as she walked that she was becoming interested and involved with Campbell's wild creatures almost in spite of herself, and she smiled as she yet again pushed back her hair against the playful tug of the wind.

It was warm, almost too warm, and as she neared the loch she noticed the clouds that had gathered around the hilltops and beamed long shafts of promised rain from their woolly blackness. Over the crags she spotted something suddenly, the soaring dark shape of the golden eagle circling like a threat against the frowning cumulus, and automatically she put a hand to shade her eyes as she watched him.

That first time when Campbell had pointed it out to her she had been impressed, but now she felt a curious sense of pride that soared with those great wings and gave her a glimpse of how Campbell must feel. The bird did not widen its field of flight but continued to circle round and round above the stark grey crags that housed its eyrie, and she recalled that Campbell had claimed that meant a storm was imminent.

The humidity, the gathering clouds and the hovering eagle were all warning signs that she would do well to heed, and she stopped short of the loch, though with some reluctance, and started to make her way back. She walked rather more quickly on the return journey with the threat of rain behind her, but the first spots came far sooner than she expected and she rued her own lack of foresight in coming without a jacket. The thin dress she was wearing would provide little protection once it started in earnest, and she would very soon become soaked, nor was there any kind of shelter between her and the bulk of Castle Eyrie standing so tauntingly on the skyline.

The wind rose too, seeming to come out of nowhere, and soon she was lashed by the fury of wind and rain, with the skirt of her dress tugging and flapping while it wrapped itself around her thighs. It impeded her progress so much that she was thoroughly out of temper and bemoaning her fate when she heard something that told her she was not the only one to have been caught.

Just as she had the day before, she turned at the drumming sound that seemed to vibrate the earth under her feet, and peered through the rain to see the grey stallion with Campbell in the saddle bearing down on her, just like yesterday. He came fast and the animal's grey coat had the glossy darkness of a seal when it was pulled up right beside her, its eyes wild with the thrill of the gallop, and the whipping storm.

This time she did not hesitate when Campbell reached down for her, but gave him both her hands. Without a word he lifted her off her feet and swung her upward, but she wasn't perched behind him in this instance, instead she was set sideways in front of him so that his body sheltered her from at least some of the storm. He needed both hands to control his mount, so Chiara put her arms around him and hung on tightly, finding it more comfortable as well as more convenient to lay her head on his shoulder.

'This is becoming a habit!' His voice was close to her ear, and she nodded without saying anything.

Just being close to him was having an effect, and the warmth of his body touched her face through the chill wetness of his shirt, sending shivers of sensation slipping along her spine. She noticed too that the skirt of her dress still clung wetly to her thighs and showed her legs to well above her knees, and it was an automatic gesture when she reached with one hand to try and pull the hem down a little.

'Don't fidget!'

The abrupt command startled her so that she snatched her hand back and once more put both arms around him, but rebellion was instinctive and she dug her fingers hard into the muscles in his back, feeling the firm flesh flinch for a moment in response. 'I was only——'

'I know what you were trying to do,' Campbell interrupted shortly, 'but don't worry about it; I've seen legs before!'

'*And* a good deal else, no doubt!'

She glanced up at him for a moment without actually raising her head, curious to see his expression. His tanned face glowed darkly with the rain and his red-gold hair was darkened and flattened to his head, giving an added harshness to the craggy features, and when he caught her eye she saw an unholy gleam in the depths of vivid blue.

'Sniper!' he said with unexpected vehemence.

There was little enough time to say anything in reply, even had she been inclined to, for the stallion had made short work of the distance and they were already clip-clopping into the cobbled yard at the rear of the castle. It was typical of him, Chiara felt, to ride straight in through the open doors of the stable building instead of dismounting in the yard, and she almost ducked her head instinctively when the horse made directly for a big straw-carpeted stall before he stopped, snorting and blowing in his relief.

Campbell swung himself down at once, then reached up for her, his big hands clasping about her waist, but something about the way he looked up at her made her decide to be independent. He hadn't forgotten that hard dig with her hands, she thought, nor the pert response to his comment about her legs.

'I can manage by myself, thank you!'

She tried to push away the helping hands at the same time as she started to slide down from the horse's back, but the manoeuvre failed to come off—partly because the stallion was much taller than she had realised and she was a lot further from the ground, and partly because Campbell was unprepared and unwilling to relinquish his hold on her. In the event she came unseated swiftly and without control, and her rapid descent caught Campbell off guard, knocking him backwards into the bristly straw with her sprawled alongside him, breathless.

Neither of them did or said anything for a moment, then Campbell swore softly and heaved on to one elbow to look down at her with eyes that gleamed between thick wet lashes. 'If that's the way you want to play it!' he muttered between tight lips, and rolled swiftly over so that she gasped aloud at the sudden pressure of his weight.

'No, Campbell!'

Her hands pushed at the broad resistance of his chest, but he wasn't easy to move, and he was angry for some reason she couldn't quite define; it showed in the passionate fierceness of his eyes. He pinioned her with his arms either side of her, his hands first gripping her shoulders tightly, then pulling at the thin stuff of her dress to expose the smoothness of her shoulders, forcing apart the front opening.

She fought hard not to succumb, but the warm hard pressure of his mouth on her neck was irresistible and she felt her body responding as if of its own accord to the vigour of his. From her neck to the pulsing softness of her throat and shoulders, his mouth moved inexorably down to the deep shadowy valley between her breasts.

Her head was filled with the drumming of her own heartbeat and the harsh sound of his breathing as he sought and found her mouth, his own more cruelly hard than she had ever known it, so fierce and demanding that she seemed to have stopped breathing, and felt herself slipping into some strange void of pulsing darkness that at last began to alarm as well as excite her.

If he had said just one word to suggest that he loved her, that he wanted her for some other reason than the purely mercenary one he had spoken of at the beginning, Chiara would have yielded without a struggle. For there was about this man something that could take her beyond the normal pleasure of kisses and lift her to ecstatic heights she had only dreamed of.

But Campbell said nothing, seeming bent only on satisfying his own passions and on venting that gleaming, inexplicable anger she had seen in his eyes. It was his silence and his lack of tenderness that made her hit out the moment he freed her mouth and she was able to breathe freely again; but she did so as much in desperation as with any real desire to hurt.

'Let me go!' she gasped in breathless haste before he silenced her again. 'I'm not Betty McDonald!'

Immediately she felt the whole long length of him stiffen and become still, and the thudding urgency of their combined heartbeats was a reminder of their closeness. For a long moment Campbell did not move, but stayed with his face buried in the wet tangle of her hair, his breath whispering warmly against her neck, and only her own laboured breathing and the snorting of the neglected stallion broke the quiet.

Even the hissing rattle of the rain on the roof seemed to have lessened and made no more than a chill shushing sound. There was no other but daylight in the stable and that was dimmed by the overcast skies outside, giving added harshness to the face that was raised suddenly and looked down at her for a moment with heavy lids half concealing the look in his eyes.

'Damn you!' Campbell swore softly, and got to his feet.

He did not even pause to look down at her again, but turned away, and Chiara was left to get up in her own time. There were no willing hands to help her, and she was shaking like a leaf as she stood brushing straw and stable dust from her bedraggled dress, filled with such a confused tangle of emotions that she could not be absolutely sure what she felt—only that somewhere in the confusion she regretted saying what she had to him.

It was almost as if he had forgotten her existence as he got on with tending his horse, and he did not even look over his shoulder at her when she stood just behind him. Instead Chiara was faced with a broad discouraging back and a glimpse of a profile so set and stern that she hesitated even to move, much less to say anything.

Free of his tack and thankful for the belated attention, the stallion was enjoying a hard rub down, and Chiara realised that for the moment the animal's needs took priority. Yet it was too difficult to just walk off without saying a word, and she couldn't bring herself to do it. With the tip of her tongue she moistened lips that still burned with the pressure of another mouth, as she moved even closer beside him.

'Campbell.' She spoke in a small husky voice that was alarmingly unsteady and waited for him to turn and look at her.

He stood sideways on to her and she wondered for a moment, when she saw his expression, if he meant to go on ignoring her and get on with what he was doing. Her own senses told her that he was as aware of her as she was of him, but it was a second or two before he responded; when he did he spoke without turning his head. 'All right, Chiara, I can see why you've had second thoughts about taking my word for it. After what just happened I suppose you've reason to believe it *could* have been me after all who——'

'No!'

She stopped him hastily, and it was quite automatic to place a hand on his arm, her fingers curved into the brown flesh that was still slightly damp. He was obliged to stop what he was doing or shake her off, and she took heart from the fact that he didn't do that, but turned to face her. There was a look in his eyes, however, that she had never seen there before and he seemed suddenly to have grown more distant so that she instinctively slid her hand away.

'But don't worry,' he went on as if she had not spoken, 'I'll not trouble you again. I'll not have you expecting to be ravished every time I get within touching distance, so I'll leave you strictly alone in future, Chiara.'

It wasn't what she wanted, she knew that, but at the moment Chiara couldn't have said exactly what it was she did want. She said nothing, only stood with one hand clasping the other arm and shrinking from the chill of her wet clothes, but her eyes were unconsciously appealing. It should be a relief to know that Campbell would no longer be pursuing her so relentlessly for the purpose of gaining the whole of Castle Eyrie when their grandfather died, but somehow it wasn't.

When he slid a hand beneath her chin suddenly she tried not to gasp aloud, and she made no effort to evade him but kept her eyes downcast and a soft, reproachful droop to her lower lip. His palm moved slightly and a thumb pulled gently at her lip, and there was a hint of his more usual buoyancy in his voice when he spoke.

'Och, away in and get out of those wet things,' he told her, 'before you catch your death!'

Her heart gave a small flutter of thankfulness and she sounded slightly breathless as she looked up at him at last, her lashes wavering between open and closed. 'What about you?'

'In a wee while,' he told her, and turned back to his horse, but as she paused in the doorway of the stable before plunging into the rain once more, he called after her. 'And I'm going to give you some riding lessons, then I'll not keep coming home like young Lochinvar with you on my saddle! Away now and get yourself dry!'

Her laughter, Chiara told herself, was sheer relief because things were back to normal; or were they? For he hadn't kissed her again.

Meeting Gavin McDonald again was awkward, and when she saw him coming towards her along the village street Chiara wasn't quite sure how to react. She was still trying to decide between polite coolness and her more normal friendly smile, when Gavin took the initiative and saved her having to make the choice.

'Good afternoon, Chiara.' That at least was encouraging, for he had been barely civil the last time they met, even though she had risked Campbell's wrath to go and warn him. 'How are you?'

He was as dour as ever, she noted, although that glimmer of appreciation was present in his eyes, and now that she had his attention it seemed too good an opportunity to miss. 'Gavin, I want you to know that what happened—the wolf getting out—was sabotage. Someone cut the mesh fencing around the compound and made a hole big enough for them to get out. Fortunately it was Old Lonesome who found it and not the rest of the pack.'

She could see from his expression that he was in two minds whether or not to believe her. 'Do you tell me that someone deliberately let the brutes out?' he asked, then immediately disclaimed the idea without giving her time to confirm it. 'Och no, who'd be that daft?'

'Someone out for revenge?' Chiara suggested, then remembering Campbell's opinion, 'Or someone trying to make trouble because they don't like the idea of the reserve being there?'

His hazel eyes narrowed sharply, and she knew he was taking up the challenge personally. 'Someone like me, do you mean?' he asked, but whatever suspicions lurked at the back of her mind, Chiara couldn't believe he was so foolhardy, and she shook her head.

'More likely someone who's a lot less intelligent,' she speculated. 'I saw whoever it was, but I didn't get a proper look, not even enough to see if it was male or female. It—whoever it was, was wearing shapeless trousers and a baggy sweater with a woolly hat pulled low, so I had no chance of identifying them at all.'

Something had struck a note with him, Chiara saw it happen, and he was suddenly evasive, not quite meeting her eyes when she looked at him, a fact that made her uneasy. 'What's going to happen?' he asked. 'Is he likely to sue whoever it is, if they're caught?'

It took her by surprise, she had to admit, and she didn't know what Campbell had in mind. 'I don't know,' she confessed.

Gavin looked frankly disbelieving. 'Oh, surely *you* know!'

Something about the way he said that made her frown, and she looked at him curiously. 'Why should you assume that I know what Campbell means to do?' she asked, and Gavin shook his head impatiently.

'Because you're as close to him as anyone is likely to be!' He caught himself up suddenly as if he had said too much, then apparently decided he had gone too far to draw back, and there was a glint of defiance in his eyes when he looked at her. 'Everyone knows what

Campbell Roberts is like with women,' he went on in a jerky and obviously embarrassed explanation. 'The fact that you're his cousin I doubt would make much difference to him!'

Chiara's heart was rapping hard and fast, but she tried hard to keep control of a rising temper, and she hoped her voice was as cool as she tried to make it. 'Whatever anyone knows—or guesses—is true about Campbell,' she told him, 'I am *not* one of his conquests, and you may tell all the gossips, whoever they are, that they've got hold of the wrong end of the stick—yet again!'

The oblique reference to the misconception that Campbell was the father of Betty McDonald's child had been irresistible, and she made no excuse for it, but Gavin's face flushed with resentment. 'There is said to be no smoke without fire,' he reminded her. 'Campbell Roberts is not as pure as the driven snow, you have said as much yourself, Chiara, but it is not his exploits I'm concerned with at this moment; it is what he is likely to be doing about whoever cut that fence.'

His self-control, Chiara recognised, was quite remarkable, for she could imagine how much he must have resented her jibe and he was not a man who would easily forget or forgive. Even so she saw him as being honest despite his shortsightedness, and because she felt as she did she answered him readily. 'I honestly don't know what he's likely to do,' she confessed. 'First it's necessary to find out who did it, and that would have to be left to the police, I imagine, then I'd say that a good deal would depend on the—the condition of whoever it was.'

'Condition?'

He took that up swiftly, Chiara noted, and nodded. 'It would have to be taken into account,' she pointed out, 'and I would say that whoever took the risk of turning a pack of wolves loose in the countryside must be at least a bit soft in the head.'

'Oh aye, aye, indeed.'

Something in his manner, in the way he looked when he said it gave her a sense of unease, and Chiara eyed him curiously. 'Gavin—do you know, or have some idea, who it could have been?'

She noticed the sudden tightening of his mouth and his eyes were evasive again, confirming her suspicion that he knew something, or at least suspected something. 'What makes you say that?' he demanded, and she hastily shook her head.

'I don't know, just—something.'

He said nothing for several moments and Chiara got the impression that he was thinking over something very carefully before he eventually came to a decision. Then he thrust out a hand and took hers, folding it tightly in strong fingers for a moment while his eyes became evasive again and slightly narrowed. 'I can mebbe help in some way,' he told her, 'but I'll thank you not to say so to Campbell Roberts, Chiara.'

She had told him once before that she was not very good at deceiving anyone and keeping secrets, and she shrugged uneasily. 'If it's anything that will help to solve the mystery,' she said, 'I don't see——'

'Will you not take my word for it that I cannot be more outright at the moment?' Gavin insisted, and when a brief and slightly bemused nod promised her silence he squeezed her fingers again before letting them go. 'Goodbye for now, Chiara, I have to go!' He had turned and was walking away from her while Chiara still stood gazing after him and wondering.

It was not until he put in an early and quite unexpected appearance at Castle Eyrie the following morning that she learned what it was all about. She and Campbell were leaving, shortly after breakfast, when Gavin McDonald drew up in the same battered old jeep he had driven in pursuit of the escaped wolf, and heaven knew what automatic reflex made Campbell reach for her hand and squeeze it firmly when he heard her catch her breath.

'Don't worry, girl,' he murmured with a trace of that wolfish grin, 'I'll not put a bullet through him!'

Gavin left the jeep and approached in a curiously stiff-legged gait that it took Chiara a moment or two to realise was sheer nervousness. Campbell took not a single step to meet him but stood on the steps and watched him come with all the inflexible arrogance of his lordly forebears, and the fingers that held hers were almost cruelly tight, but she did nothing to ease them at the moment.

'Good morning.' At least Campbell spared him the first approach. 'What brings you here, Gavin?'

It was somewhat surprising to hear him use a first name, and it made her wonder about relations before things went wrong between them. Gavin gave her a swift and not altogether happy glance, then placed a booted foot on the lowest step and pushed the tweed hat he wore to the back of his head.

'I'd like a word,' he said.

Campbell was half-turned, a hand extended invitingly. 'Come——'

'Out here will do fine,' Gavin assured him quickly, and Campbell eyed him narrowly for a moment over his shoulder, then shrugged and turned back to resume that lordly stance on the steps.

'It's about the animal you shot yesterday,' he guessed, and Gavin nodded shortly.

He was out of his element, it seemed to Chiara, and she felt sorry for him without knowing why he was there or how much he knew about the escape. 'Did Chiara—Miss Manti say anything about seeing me yesterday afternoon?'

Campbell's brows winged swiftly upward and he regarded him with a faint smile that could have done nothing for the other man's confidence. 'Why should Chiara tell me who she meets while she's out?' he questioned. 'Did you give her a message to bring me?'

'Oh no, I just thought that——' Gavin shrugged and thrust both hands into his pockets. 'I was wondering if you were of a mind to prosecute whoever it was that cut the wire of your wolf enclosure.'

'You know who cut it?'

Gavin looked at him straight for a moment and there was a bright angry colour in his face as he anticipated, just as he had the previous day with Chiara. 'It wasn't me!'

'I know that, man, for God's sake!' Campbell told him shortly. 'You may be all kinds of a fool, but you'd not risk losing your flock by letting my wolf pack loose!' His eyes narrowed and he had never looked more overwhelmingly powerful than he did to Chiara's bemused eyes at that moment. 'But you want my word for it that there'll be no prosecution before you tell me who *did* cut the wire.' It was not a question but a flat statement, and Gavin glanced at him warily. But Campbell, it seemed, needed no telling. 'Betty,' he said softly, and Chiara blinked in surprise.

Gavin's face was flushed and his eyes had a bright defensive look; his hands, Chiara noticed, were tightly clenched at his side, as if he held his emotions firmly in check. 'She—doesn't always see things straight,' he explained in a harsh tight voice that touched Chiara's heart. 'Not since the boy was born.'

'Three years is a hell of a long time to wait!' Campbell remarked in a voice far more chill than the compassion that showed in his eyes.

Gavin shrugged, and it was clear that he found the telling much harder than he had anticipated. 'It was with hearing the rumour,' he went on. 'She'd heard in the village that you and——' He indicated Chiara with a wave of his hand. 'However true or not, it affected her, and then hearing me talking about those murderous brutes roaming about up there and a danger to all and sundry . . .'

'She took matters into her own hands,' Campbell guessed dryly, and Gavin could only nod his agreement.

'Do you *know* she did, Gavin?' Both men turned and looked at her as if they had forgotten she was there, and she darted a swift, anxious glance at Campbell's stern face. 'I just—wondered.'

'Aye, I know she did,' Gavin confirmed, though with obvious reluctance. 'When I learned that the wire fence had been cut I remembered seeing Betty coming back to the house a couple of days ago with the wire-cutters in her hand. I took no notice at the time, for she's a way of fixing any bit of fencing that gets broken in case the laddie gets out and gets lost. She was dressed just as Chiara said, in trousers that are too big for her since she lost so much weight, and an old sweater. I didn't notice a hat, but she might have had it in her pocket by then; she'd not want me to be too curious, you see.'

'And was she out the night before too?'

Apparently the question was unexpected, and Gavin glanced first at Chiara before he answered him. 'I don't know,' he confessed. 'I was over to Hamish Grieve's for about an hour and a half.' His eyes darted between the two of them, seeking some new trial for his patience. 'Why would you be asking that?'

'Just that we saw someone dash across the road from the forest when we were on our way back from Kerside,' Campbell explained. 'Maybe it's as well we came along when we did, or it might have been the whole pack that got out and with the whole night to go on the rampage.'

'I seldom leave her alone at night,' said Gavin, and shook his head, as if he found it all too much for him suddenly. 'You'll not be taking her to court, Campbell?'

Again the use of the christian name was unexpected, and Chiara began to wonder just how friendly the two men might have been at one time. 'I'll not take her to court,' Campbell promised. 'But you'd best keep a closer eye on her, for I cannot promise to be so lenient next time.'

Gavin flushed, and he resented the warning, that was clear, but he was for the moment too relieved on his sister's behalf to make a point of it. 'There'll be no next time,' he vowed. 'She's away to Edinburgh to see a special doctor next week, and——'

His brief shrug was alarmingly affecting, and Chiara wondered if Campbell had been touched by it. She had her answer when he proffered his hand, and Gavin rather bemusedly took it. 'It'll be a good thing,' he told him 'Better for all of you when she gets straightened out. I'm glad you came,' he went on, looking Gavin directly in the eye, 'because I know you could have kept quiet and I'd never have been the wiser. I'm glad you didn't.'

Gavin said nothing, and Chiara wondered if perhaps he was too relieved that the interview he must have dreaded had turned out better than he dared hope. But he was a dour and unbending man, as Campbell had said, and he returned to his battered vehicle, then drove off without a backward glance while Chiara still stood on the steps and watched him go.

'Cam——'

'Don't call me that,' he told her quietly but without taking his eyes off the departing jeep, 'I don't like it.'

'But Grandpa and Uncle——'

'I'm too well brought up to argue with my father and my grandfather,' he informed her flatly, 'but you I *can* put right!' He turned and looked down at her suddenly with a bright gleaming look in his eyes. 'Women!' he declared forcefully, and took her hand again, crushing her fingers in a steely grip.

Chiara walked down the steps with him to the Land Rover, and she guessed something of what was going on in his mind. 'You fell out over Betty,' she guessed, and a brief jerky nod of his head admitted the truth of her guess. 'Because Gavin believes that boy is yours?'

'Because she told him so, and who else would he believe!' He let go her hand and saw her into the Land Rover, but still stood beside it, musing rather than talking to her, she thought. 'He's as straightlaced as a Victorian spinster, always was even as a boy, and like most of his kind he's ready to believe the worst of anyone who's already in his words, a bit of a rake.'

'He said that?'

From the way his eyes gleamed it was hard to believe he had resented it. 'Give a dog a bad name,' he quoted with a sardonic hint of smile, 'and it was a McDonald woman that was the eventual cause of that notorious ancestor I mentioned being sent to the States. I could live with the name he called me, however undeserved, but what I wouldn't swallow was being given a lecture about my licentious ways before anyone else even knew the wretched girl was pregnant, and when he supposed I might be considering putting them off the farm because of it——'

'Oh no!' She looked up at him, scarcely believing it. 'He can't have known you very well, that's all I can say!'

The tightness of his mouth eased suddenly and he smiled down at her with the familiar gleam of mockery in his eyes. 'I think you just said something nice about me,' he warned her. 'Better be careful, girl, or you might get into the habit!'

He was laughing as he turned away and he waved a careless hand as he went off round to the stable for his horse. As Chiara started up the engine she realised that he hadn't even attempted to kiss her before he went, and she wished she didn't miss it so much.

CHAPTER SIX

CHIARA and her grandfather had sat for quite a long time in the big sitting-room downstairs just chatting about this and that, and the situation was not really to her aunt's liking. She made it obvious by looking across at them every so often as if she suspected their subject of conversation, although she could have missed very little of what was being said from where she was sitting.

Whether or not Campbell had told his grandfather about Betty McDonald being the culprit who had damaged the wolf compound, Chiara had no idea, but at the moment she was giving him her version. 'It seemed to me that they knew one another pretty well,' she told him, referring to the two men using one another's first names, and the old man smiled.

'They were very good friends at one time,' he agreed. 'When they were laddies and Tom McDonald had Brae Farm, the two of them were inseparable, although Campbell is a year or two older. They just never did see eye to eye on matters of conservation, though, even before they really knew what the word meant and before it became the big move it is now. Young Gavin saw it from the farmers' viewpoint, of course, and could see no advantage at all in bringing back the creatures that had made life hazardous for his forebears.'

'It was the animals that started it, then?'

Something in her voice caught her grandfather's attention, and he eyed her curiously for a moment. 'That was the beginning of it, I believe,' he agreed quietly, and glanced for a second only at his daughter-in-law before he went on, his voice slightly lowered. 'That business of

Betty was later on, and what you might call the last straw.'

Chiara traced along the arm of her chair with a finger-tip, choosing her words with care, partly because she felt sure Aunt Margaret could hear, and partly because she wasn't entirely sure of her grandfather's feelings in the matter. 'Campbell told me about it,' she said, 'and I said Gavin couldn't have known him very well if he thought Campbell would deny his own son.'

'Good for you, my dear!' her grandfather approved, but Margaret Roberts snorted her disgust, her flat voice intruding into their quiet conversation.

'Only a fool would believe such a story! No one who knows my son would believe him capable of doing such a despicable thing, but mud sticks, and that wretched woman told so many lies that there are still some who accept her word for it!'

'Gavin does,' Chiara affirmed, 'but of course he's bound to be loyal to his sister. If she says the boy is Campbell's he can't really do other than believe her.'

'As if he would have anything to do with a creature like that!' her aunt declared in disgust, and Chiara felt that had Campbell done as Betty McDonald wanted and married her, she would have been much more sorry even than she was now.

'There was a precedent, of course,' the old man mused, with a hint of mischief in his eyes for a moment, and the words were evidently indistinguishable to Margaret in this instance, for she did not rise to them, only gave him a long suspicious look before returning to her needle-work. 'I suppose you've heard about John Roberts?' he asked, and Chiara nodded.

'Campbell told me. He suggested I was giving him credit for a similar reputation.'

'And were you?'

'Not exactly,' she demurred, and her grandfather laughed.

So far she had said nothing to him about Campbell's proposal to her for his own mercenary reasons, and she wondered if he knew about it. She could not even begin to guess, she realised, what the old man's reaction was likely to be if he didn't already know, and she was very tempted to tell him, just to see what kind of a response she got.

'He'll not get his own way with you, I'll guarantee,' her grandfather speculated, his faded eyes watching her closely. 'Not too easily, at least,' he added slyly, and shook his head when she coloured. 'I wonder you don't learn to ride, my dear; you'd look fine on a horse and you could keep Campbell company instead of racketing around the place in that damned noisy wagon thing.'

Chiara smiled; she knew her grandfather's dislike of motorised vehicles of any kind being used around the estate, however useful they were. 'I'd find it very difficult carrying a load of hay on the back of a horse, Grandpa,' she told him, 'and that's mostly what I use the Land Rover for.'

'Noisy damned thing,' the old man insisted, determinedly contrary. 'And I still don't see why it should stop you from learning to ride, there's a lot more pleasure to be had on the back of a good horse than driving around in a motor vehicle.'

'Campbell did offer to teach me at one time,' Chiara told him, and the old man eyed her quizzically.

'Then why didn't you, child?'

She shrugged, smoothing imaginary creases from her skirt and aware that Margaret Roberts was once more taking an interest. 'Oh, I don't know, I suppose he had second thoughts, probably.'

'And he has quite enough to do without giving riding lessons,' her aunt observed tartly from her place by the window, but her father-in-law gave her a resigned half-smile.

'Nothing a healthy young blood like Cam can't cope

with, Margaret,' he told her, and looked again at Chiara's slightly flushed face. 'And I'll not believe he'd count teaching a pretty girl to ride as much of a chore! You must mention it to him again, Chiara; he mebbe thinks you're not keen, so he hasn't said any more about it.'

'In a way I'm not too keen,' Chiara confessed. 'I quite like the sensation, but I don't altogether fancy being perched so far from the ground with nothing to hold on to but reins.'

'You never were afraid when you were a wee girl,' her grandfather reminded her. 'Why don't you give it a try, Chiara, and see how you like being high enough up to see all around you?'

'I have and I do,' Chiara proclaimed swiftly and without pausing to think. 'Only I fancy it would be very different perched up there on my own without Campbell to hold on to!'

'Oh, aye, I dare say.' The old man spoke softly and with stress on that gentle accent, but his eyes gleamed with interest; as his daughter-in-law's did, but for a different reason. 'And you will be speaking from the point of view of experience, I don't doubt.'

Chiara saw where the subject had led her and felt oddly shy suddenly when she met those bright, curious eyes, because they were so much like those of the man they were discussing. 'Oh, he's brought me home a couple of times,' she told him, deceptively airy. 'Campbell calls it rescuing me, for want of a better term. Once was when the Land Rover ran out of petrol, and the second time was when I got caught in a storm and was soaked through to the skin.'

'A knight in shining armour, eh?' her grandfather suggested, then chuckled in a way that implied he had reservations about his grandson's form of gallantry, and Chiara pursed a doubtful lip.

'I don't know about that,' she demurred. 'He's complained on both occasions about my being a nuisance, so

I don't think gallantry had a lot to do with it. That was when he said he'd teach me to ride, to save him the trouble of having to keep rescuing me.'

'Och, that's just his way,' old Ian assured her confidently. 'Cam's man enough to enjoy rescuing pretty girls, and you shouldn't take him seriously, child!'

He caught his breath as he finished speaking and Chiara thought he looked a little paler, but he was still smiling and a swift glance in her direction suggested that her aunt had noticed nothing amiss. 'I might take him up on it one day,' she said. But thinking about the last time Campbell had made the suggestion recalled that he had only a moment before promised never to trouble her further with his plan to marry her, and something of what was going on in her mind must have shown on her face, for the old man looked at her with his head to one side, gently quizzical.

'You've not been quarrelling with him, have you, Chiara?' he asked, and Chiara shrugged uncertainly, wondering if he did know anything about that controversial proposal of marriage.

'Only about the same old thing,' she told him, and cast her aunt a brief wary look before she went on, 'and I don't suppose that will arise again now. It—it was something that Campbell asked me—no, *told* me, just after I first came here. I turned it down flat and I've been doing so ever since, though until recently he's never taken me seriously.'

'Do you mean about marrying you?' the old man asked, so matter-of-factly that Chiara stared at him for a moment in blank disbelief.

'You know about it and you're not—shocked?'

'Och, now why would I be shocked at the idea of a man wanting to marry a girl as pretty as yourself?' her grandfather demanded, and it was obvious that he saw nothing amiss with the idea at all.

Chiara took a deep breath and there was a bright flush

in her cheeks as she prepared to argue her point. 'I can think of several reasons,' she told him. 'For one thing because we're first cousins——'

'Not full first cousins,' her grandfather interrupted firmly, 'there's no bar there, girl!'

'And for another because he wants to marry me simply to get his hands on the whole of Castle Eyrie,' Chiara insisted desperately. 'I find that not only horribly mercenary, but—insulting too!'

Her grandfather was given no opportunity to reply in that instance, for Margaret Roberts spoke up swiftly and forcefully, her gaunt face flushed and her eyes gleaming indignantly. 'And how else would he get what is rightfully his?' she demanded. 'It would not have been necessary if things had been allocated as they should have been, instead of being given to an outsider; someone who has never spent more than a few weeks here in her life! Campbell had a mind to marry Mary Bannen until he found that unless he married you he would be losing half of what should rightfully be his.'

But old Ian would have none of that. His voice was a little shakier and his colour was high, but he asserted the authority he had held for more than half a century with as much force as he had always done. 'Nonsense, woman!' he told Margaret. 'Cam's no more of a mind to marry that prissy little creature than I am, he's too much sense! As for what should or should not be his is for me to decide when the times comes, and I've a mind to live a while longer yet!'

His insistence had its effect, but the old man was breathing very heavily as he glared across at his daughter-in-law, who sat with her eyes downcast and obviously regretting her outburst. 'Indeed you will,' she told him, but with unexpected warmth in her voice, for Chiara had noticed before how much well-concealed affection there was between these two such opposing characters. Looking up from her sewing, her grey eyes gleamed at him for a moment. 'You're too wicked an old man to go too soon, God help us!'

She seemed to notice the change in him for the first time, and was already getting to her feet while the old man chuckled breathlessly at her reply, and Chiara got up too, startled by the change in his appearance. 'Grandpa, are you all right?'

He had a hand to his chest and he was obviously in pain and having difficulty in breathing, while Margaret loosened the collar of his shirt a little more and pressed him back in his chair. 'It will pass,' she told Chiara quietly, and seemed to know exactly what she was doing. 'I'll fetch him his medicine; stay with him until I come back, Chiara, and don't let him move.'

The old man opened his eyes and looked rather dazedly at Chiara's anxious face bending over him, and he attempted a smile. 'I'm fine, girl,' he told her in a thin faint voice. 'Don't worry about it. I'll be fine in just a few moments, you'll see.'

'You will stay quiet and not talk,' Margaret told him firmly as she crossed the room, and she could not resist a parting shot just before she left them. 'And you would be much better to rest instead of getting yourself into such a state, Father Roberts, as well you know. Sit back now and close your eyes for a wee while till I fetch your medicine for you.'

Chiara had never heard that harsh voice so soothing as when she chided the old man, and it reaffirmed her suspicion that Margaret Roberts was very genuinely fond of her father-in-law. To Chiara her grandfather looked very much more like he had the day she arrived at Castle Eyrie, so that she began to suspect he might recently have recovered from a similar attack in that instance too, and she looked down at him anxiously until he opened his eyes again and smiled at her.

'I'm just getting old, child,' he whispered, and Chiara put a warning finger to her lips, advice that he ignored. 'Don't take Margaret at face value either, Chiara, she's a good woman for all her sour tongue, and I'd not manage without her.'

Chiara, ever emotional when people she cared for were concerned, caught her lip between her teeth and determinedly swallowed the tears that threatened. 'Oh, Grandpa, if I could——'

'Och, now don't go sentimental on me!' the old man told her in a voice that already sounded stronger. 'I'm feeling better already, and the tablet Margaret is bringing me will set me up fine. But I will rest for a while, so why don't you go and find Campbell, eh?'

'Not until Aunt Margaret comes back with your tablet,' she said, recalling her aunt's injunction.

He was smiling as if her insistence amused him, and there was certainly a little more natural colour in his face, a little more alertness in the faded blue eyes. Chiara half-turned her head when she heard Margaret returning, and her grandfather's hand was placed in the small of her back as she turned right around, as if he would insist on her leaving him.

'Go and find young Campbell,' he told her huskily, 'and tell him I said he's to make you smile!'

She left him when Margaret took over, bringing a glass of water and a tablet that she carried in a twist of paper. It was a task she had obviously performed many times before, and Chiara was prepared to let her take charge since she knew exactly what she was doing, and sickness of any kind gave Chiara a curiously helpless feeling.

Having no real idea where she might find Campbell, but automatically obeying her grandfather's directive, she made for the stable and found him there hefting bales of hay from one place to another with a pitchfork. He looked hot and dirty and he frowned at her curiously, brushing a forearm across his brow when he saw her coming. He stuck the fork into a pile of hay bales and stood watching her, obviously intrigued by her unusually sober expression.

'Why so gloomy?' he asked, and Chiara flopped down on to one of the bales before she said anything.

'I was looking for you.'

Campbell nudged her along and sat beside her, again brushing a forearm across his brow. He was hot and he smelled of hay as well as the more earthy smell of hard labour, and his nearness was infinitely disturbing, Chiara found. Resting his elbows on his knees, he leaned forward, and the arm that touched hers was warm and smooth and slightly damp, the heat from his body seeming to envelop her with his earthy virility and making it hard for her to think clearly.

Snatching herself back to earth, she hugged her knees while she enlightened him. 'Grandpa said I should come and find you,' she told him, and although she smiled when he turned and looked at her, the concern she felt showed in her eyes. 'He said to tell you to make me smile.'

'Did he?' He spoke quietly and continued watching her after she had averted her own gaze. 'And why do you need to be made to smile, eh? Has Mother been getting at you, or have you been up to something you shouldn't and come a cropper?'

For once she ignored his attempt to bait her and sat for a moment with a strand of hay between her fingers, twisting it restlessly in and out until a large hand reached over and clasped them tightly, squeezing encouragingly when she looked up for a moment. 'I—I was talking to Grandpa and he had some kind of attack.'

The hand over hers gripped almost painfully tight for a second, and Campbell was already half-risen when she shook her head at him. 'How bad, Chiara?'

'I—I don't know.' She moistened her lips anxiously, and the hand over hers was very reassuring somehow. 'Grandpa says he'll be right as rain when he's had his tablet, and certainly he seemed better even before Aunt Margaret brought it for him.'

'It happens,' he said, and somehow his quietness seemed to have an air of finality so that she looked up swiftly with an appeal in her eyes. 'He has these attacks every so often,' he went on to explain, 'and there's really nothing anyone can do except make sure he takes it easy for a while and stays quiet. Not that it's very easy to achieve with Grandpa, he's a game old boy and he'll not lie down and become an invalid for anyone. Though he's as good as gold with my mother as a rule.'

'She's very good with him,' Chiara said, unhesitatingly giving praise where it was due. 'And they like one another.'

'You sound surprised,' Campbell told her with a faint grin. 'It's because Mother gives him as good as he gives, and Grandpa always enjoys a good battle; he's a real old Roberts!'

'Like you!' Chiara retorted, and he looked at her for a moment, then gave her a brief and faintly sardonic smile as he got to his feet.

'Like me,' he agreed, and reached for her hands, drawing her up until she stood facing him, and folding his strong brown fingers over hers. 'I shall miss sparring with you,' he told her, and something in the blue eyes stirred little thrills of excitement that fluttered over her skin like cool fingers. Then he shook his head and kept hold of one hand while they walked across the stable yard. 'I've something here to make you smile—come and see.'

The stable door stood open as it most often did, and to Chiara it was automatic to remember the last time she had been there; dripping wet and insisting on getting down from the grey stallion's back without Campbell's assistance. Her heart was thudding wildly as she walked into the semi-gloom with him, for it was much too easy to recall exactly how it had felt to be crushed by that lean body and kissed by the mouth that now merely smiled faintly, as if at some secret thought.

The straw rustled under their feet and the restless thud of hooves on the floor suggested that the occupants recognised Campbell's voice and anticipated an outing. 'What—what is it you're going to show me?' she asked, trying to banish those disturbing thoughts from her mind, and he lightly tapped the end of her nose with a forefinger.

'You'll see,' he told her. 'Something you've never seen before, I'll bet, and mebbe won't again.'

He took her into an empty stall, and once more her thoughts went back to that stormy interlude only such a short time ago. Next door the stallion stirred restlessly and reminded them of his presence, but Campbell was crouching down beside a smallish wooden box that stood in one corner of the empty stall. It was faced with fine wire mesh and she couldn't see what it contained.

Standing back a little, Chiara waited, wondering what it was he had. She looked at him curiously and noticed he was smiling in that oddly secretive way he had while he donned a pair of thick leather gloves before lifting the mesh and reaching inside.

What he brought out cradled in his big hands looked like an ordinary tabby kitten at first sight, a kitten with bright yellow eyes; but even before she instinctively reached out to it, he uttered a warning. 'Don't touch it!'

She drew back just in time, for the tiny creature lashed out viciously and its pink mouth gaped in a hissing snarl that was startlingly aggressive and showed baby teeth that already looked needle-sharp. It dug its claws into the gloves Campbell had put on and she could see why he had taken the precaution of wearing them, for even at that age the animal was obviously capable of inflicting quite a nasty wound.

In fact the little creature's fighting spirit seemed to amuse him, for he was laughing as he held it in front of him and looked directly into the kittenish face that glared defiance at him, its ears flat and spitting at him furiously. 'Isn't she a little beauty?' he asked delightedly, and laughed again when the kitten lashed out at his face, just out of reach. 'And you're a bonny scrapper too, aren't you? You'd have my eyes out as soon as look at me!'

'Campbell, be careful! If it does catch your eyes——'

'I'm not daft enough to give her the chance,' Campbell assured her, and lowered his hands so that she could see the kitten better.

Chiara was tempted. She liked cats and this one was pretty, for all its determined aggression, though it was painfully thin and its head looked far too big for its body. She would love to have stroked it, for the boldly striped fur looked downy soft, but having seen what it could do she kept her distance while she admired it.

'Is it a real wildcat?'

'The genuine article,' Campbell assured her, very obviously fascinated with his captive. 'It's about four or five weeks old, I would guess, and an orphan as far as we can tell; that's why it's here, I'd not bring a wild thing in and cage it otherwise. Another few weeks and it will be able to take care of itself, but for the moment it needs someone to care for it.'

'What happened to the mother, do you think?'

She watched him lightly stroke a finger down the kitten's back and caught her breath when he received another swipe from those vicious claws as a reward. Something about his gentleness and his amusement at the tiny animal's fury struck unexpected chords in her, and she felt somehow more close to understanding him suddenly. In another setting he could be a cultured and even a sophisticated man, although the sophistication was no more than a veneer, she thought, yet here, in this more basic environment, he had an almost uncanny closeness to the wild creatures he cared for, and the enigma of the real man intrigued her.

He placed the kitten carefully back in its box and fastened the mesh over the front again, then turned to smile at her as he drew off his gloves. 'I found it by the loch this morning when I went out first thing. There was another a bit further on, obviously drowned, and no sign of an adult female, and as this scrap looked like ending up like her twin I scooped her up in my jacket and brought her home. She was wet and hungry but still ready to take on all comers, whether they had good intentions or not. You'll know what I mean,' he added with a look that left her in no doubt of the comparison he was making. 'Some females just don't appreciate being rescued.'

Determinedly ignoring the allusion, Chiara kept her eyes on the kitten and did her best to stop her voice betraying how she felt. 'What will you do with it?' she asked. 'I mean, how do you care for wildcats?'

Campbell shrugged. 'I leave that part of it to Murdoch,' he told her, and again made it clear that he was making comparisons. 'He has more luck taming wildcats than I do; I just don't seem to have the right touch for handling kittens who are determinedly unfriendly.'

In no doubt at all that he was alluding to her own implacable rejection of him, Chiara fought to keep her voice from sounding husky, but she determinedly refused to take up the challenge he offered. 'Is it possible to tame them?'

He was standing very close and that irresistible aura of masculinity was affecting her senses the way it always did. It was incredible how much she wanted him to reach out and touch her, and some wild and uncontrollable need for him burned in her like fire, making her feel alarmingly vulnerable. But he kept his distance where once he would have made it an opportunity to put an arm around her and kiss her, and it seemed he had at last taken her rejection of him as final, although possibly much less readily than his manner suggested.

'It's very occasionally possible to tame one,' he told her, 'but I'm not really in favour of it because to me their wildness is half their beauty. The only problem is,' he added softly and with unmistakable meaning, 'I'm aye fond of playing with a pretty kitten sometimes and I don't relish getting attacked for my trouble. I just don't seem to have the knack—with some kittens, at least.'

Chiara's heart was clamouring, beating so hard she could scarcely hear anything else, and she looked up at him uncertainly. 'Campbell——'

'Don't worry, Chiara,' he told her quietly, 'I shan't break my word!' He glanced at his wrist-watch and clucked his tongue. 'And will you look at the time! With one thing and the other there's half the morning gone and I've still not shifted this hay.'

He turned and Chiara followed him outside, the kitten's mewing cries rising to a yowl of frustration behind them. 'Can I help?' she offered, but Campbell shook his head.

He retrieved the pitchfork he had abandoned and stood for a moment looking down at her and smiling faintly. 'I don't need any help, thanks, but Murdoch can probably find you something to do if you ask him.'

'Oh yes—yes, of course.'

The very obvious dismissal hurt far more than she could have anticipated, and she wondered how he could be so heedless of what she was feeling, or why it should matter so much to her that she was being dismissed. She stood for a moment watching him while he returned to pitching hay, for clearly he had no intention of wasting any more time. What she did not understand was her own reluctance to accept a situation that she should surely have welcomed.

When he did not turn his head again, she sighed inwardly in resignation and turned away, swinging round swiftly when he called after her. 'And don't worry yourself sick about Grandpa,' he warned. 'It will do no good, girl.'

Her mouth trembled and all the tangle of emotions that churned inside her rose up and stuck like a lump in her throat, for whether or not he touched her physically the look in his eyes was gentle and understanding and it was almost her undoing. 'Campbell, I didn't——'

'Away now and give Murdoch a hand,' Campbell interrupted softly, and returned to what he was doing before she had time to be certain he was smiling.

It was just about a week after that that Chiara saw Gavin McDonald again, and when he saw her coming it was easy to guess that he was unsure of how to approach her. Chiara suspected that his sister's mental state was as much an embarrassment to him as the birth of her child had been, and she felt sorry for him as well as having a genuine liking for him.

To ease the way for him she smiled as they got nearer and asked after his sister, pausing in the middle of the cobbled footpath as if she had every intention of stopping to talk. His austerely good-looking features looked cool and withdrawn as if he would have preferred not to have the matter raised, but he answered her readily enough. He was as proud a man in his way as Campbell was, she guessed, and Betty had made him a subject of public sympathy on more than one occasion.

'She's getting along very well,' he replied. 'I thank you for asking, Chiara.'

'I expect you miss her a lot,' Chiara guessed, not quite knowing what to say or how much sympathy to show, 'you and little Robert. How is Robert?'

He did not like being drawn, that much was obvious from the expression on his face, and he seemed to be keeping his sights on some spot immediately behind her rather than look at her directly. 'Oh, he's well enough,' he allowed, 'though he misses his mother, of course. But I've a woman coming in to clean and cook and she takes care of the lad as well, so there are no problems there.'

Almost as if he feared she might suggest helping out herself, and wanted to forestall anything of the kind. In fact it did not even occur to Chiara that she could be of use in that direction, but she was impulsive and she was driven to end a rather uneasy silence, hoping to make him unbend a little.

'I'm truly sorry about it, Gavin, and no one really blames Betty for what she did. Campbell understands that she was—unwell.'

'Does he now?' His eyes had a stubborn unyielding look that she had hoped to banish completely, but after a moment or two he shook his head and there was a suggestion of weariness in his sudden resignation. 'Och, what's the use of placing blame?' he sighed. 'That kind of situation needs two, and Betty was no bairn even four years ago. She had always a fancy for Campbell Roberts, but he'd not look at her, or so it seemed. She'd not have put up much of a fight when he eventually did decide he found her attractive, I can't deny it.'

'But Campbell *does* deny it, Gavin, and I believe him.'

It was not the kind of situation she had sought to precipitate, but it was done now, and she wondered if Campbell would thank her for it in the long run. According to him there were contenders enough for Betty Mc-

Donald's favours, and her brother must surely have been aware of it, therefore he probably quite genuinely believed that her child could be Campbell's as easily as anyone else's.

Gavin's eyes had a deep dark look that she wasn't sure she could understand, but that he had a doubt, however minute and uncertain, was a progressive step, or so Chiara told herself. 'Are you telling me that my sister lied to me?' he asked. 'That I should take your word for it that Campbell Roberts——'

'Gavin, it—it just isn't him! You know him, or you did once, I'm sure of it, and you must know that he frankly admits he has a penchant for redheads, so why should he deny knowing Betty? Wouldn't you have known if she'd finally managed to—attract him? Wouldn't she have boasted about it, if she had such a fancy for him as you say? And knowing Campbell as well as I'm sure you do, can you honestly see him ducking a responsibility like that? He didn't—know her, Gavin.'

She felt herself a better advocate than she had realised, and although Gavin said nothing for a moment, she guessed it was because he was being torn two ways at once. She again felt pity for him in his dilemma and it showed in her eyes, and when he eventually heaved a sigh of resignation she believed it was because he knew he had her sympathy.

'I'm not sure what to believe,' he confessed, 'but you're a good one to have on one's side, Chiara. Mebbe when Betty comes home and she's—more herself, she'll tell what really happened.'

'I'm sure she will,' Chiara assured him readily. 'In the meantime, Gavin, is there anything she needs? Something I can send in for her that she especially likes?'

'I think not—thank you.' He was not prepared to unbend that far, but Chiara took heart from the fact that he showed a shadow of a smile on that sternly set mouth for a moment when he looked at her. 'I'm glad not to have quarrelled with you over this, Chiara, because I'd not have been at all happy about that.'

'Nor would I,' she told him with a smile. 'But why should we two quarrel? Strictly speaking it isn't really our fight, is it?'

'No-o-o.' He drawled the denial in his soft accent, and then touched her hand with his fingertips; not too obvious a gesture but one that had her attention. 'Will you come out with me one evening, Chiara?'

Coming so unexpectedly after the other matter, and seeing how anxious he looked, there was little she could do but accept. Really, she told herself, there was no reason why she shouldn't go out with him. 'Why—yes, I'd like to very much.'

'There's a little Italian restaurant in Kerside,' Gavin pressed on, anxious to persuade her she had done right. 'You'd like to eat there, I'm sure, would you not?'

How could she spoil his pleasure? He need never know that she had been there before with Campbell and he was obviously pleased to be able to take her. 'I'd love it,' she told him with a smile. 'That's very thoughtful of you, Gavin.'

He actually flushed with pleasure, and his hazel eyes gleamed like agates between their pale lashes. 'You'll mebbe have to guide me through the menu,' he told her with one of his rare smiles. 'I'll pick you up about seven tomorrow evening, if that will suit you.'

'Perfectly!'

'It will do Campbell Roberts good to discover that he is not the only fish in the sea!' he declared with what she suspected was malicious satisfaction, and the fact that he was no more kindly disposed towards Campbell gave her a few uneasy moments as she drove home.

It was quite pointless and a complete waste of a pleasant

evening, Chiara realised, to keep hoping nothing would happen to betray the fact that she had been to the same restaurant before with Campbell, but still the possibility niggled at the back of her mind every so often.

The meal was excellent and, having imbibed quite a quantity of wine, Gavin was more talkative than she had seen him before. It also brought a bold gleam to his eyes and made him smile more often, so that she wondered if she was seeing something of the man who normally lurked beneath that rather austere exterior. Only when it came time to drive home did Chiara feel any doubt about his ability, although he assured her that he was capable of driving the route blindfold.

His car was almost as aged as the jeep used around the farm, but it was shiningly clean and well cared for and it coped well with the steep and winding road back to Roberts' Brae and Castle Eyrie, until they were about half-way home. Then a minor misjudgment on a very sharp bend caused them to hit the banked side of the road with a thud that jolted the car to a halt and jerked Chiara back in her seat.

Because she had had her head turned to look out of the window, the movement banged her forehead against the window frame and for just a moment after the car stalled she felt dazed and alarmed. The familiar silence that fell after the engine stopped was reassuring in a way, and she snatched herself back to awareness when Gavin spoke.

'Are you all right?' he enquired anxiously, and she nodded, then immediately afterwards put a hand to her forehead. 'Did you bump your head? Is it bad?'

'It's only a small bump,' she assured him, warned by the tone of his voice, and looked at his slightly bemused face in the ghostly green light on the dashboard. 'Are *you* all right?'

He nodded, then obviously suffered the same regret

she had and winced as he put a hand to his head. 'Jings, my head feels like a kettledrum! I should never have had so much wine; I'm not a drinker and I *never* drink wine.'

Chiara smiled ruefully, guessing how he felt. 'Italian wines aren't as innocuous as some people expect,' she told him. 'Do you feel like driving the rest of the way, Gavin, or shall I take over?'

'Are you any more sober than I am?' he challenged, then put up a hand by way of apology. 'No, of course you're more accustomed to it; but I'm fine, Chiara— don't worry, I'll get us home.'

It seemed an interminable time, however, before he managed to get the engine restarted, and Chiara was on the point of suggesting that she walk back to a garage they had passed about a mile back when his efforts were rewarded. Breathing a gusty sigh of relief, Gavin climbed in and gave her a long steady look before he released the brake.

'O.K.?' he enquired, and Chiara thought he sounded anxious.

'O.K.,' she assured him, but took a surreptitious glance at her watch as they got under way again; it had been close on half an hour.

They had been much later than she expected leaving the restaurant, for Gavin had seemed unwilling to bring the occasion to an end, and now that they had been de-layed further while he fixed the car it was already way past the time she had expected to be home, and they still had a half-hour drive ahead of them. It wasn't that she was expected to observe a curfew that troubled her, but remembering that the same kind of date with Camp-bell had taken much less time, and someone would be wondering where she had got to. Though she didn't specify who, even in her own mind.

Lights still burned in the windows as they drove up

the approach road, but most were on the upper floor. Only one, apart from the outside light over the steps, still remained on downstairs, and Chiara would have staked her life on who it was who waited up for her, although she didn't say as much to Gavin.

Somehow she didn't expect Gavin to kiss her, and yet that was just what he did as she leaned to open the car door; a light chaste salute on her cheek. She half turned and smiled vaguely at him, then got out and turned to speak to him, but by then he was sitting straight behind the wheel again, looking rather unnaturally stiff and slightly embarrassed, judging by appearances.

'Goodnight, Gavin.'

She spoke softly, and thought she caught a glimpse of someone move in the windows of the sitting-room. She was tempted in the circumstances to lean across and return Gavin's kiss with interest, but that would have been a little unfair, so she simply smiled and gave him a brief wave before she closed the car door.

No one was at the sitting-room window when she turned to go in, but she was certain it had been Campbell who had been there, and she made directly for the sitting-room, looking across at him with bright challenging dark eyes as she opened the door.

'Had a good time?' he asked, very quietly, and she nodded, the slight movement reminding her that it could well have ended much less pleasantly than it began.

'You needn't have waited up for me, Campbell.'

'No problem,' he told her, coolly offhand. 'But there are no dances you could have gone to on a Friday night, and you were a hell of a long time over a friendly dinner; something could have gone wrong.'

His concern, she felt certain, was genuine enough, but he concealed it with that rather offhand manner, and she replied likewise. 'Oh, we had a bit of trouble with the car and it delayed us for a while, that's all.'

'What did he hit?'

The look she saw in his eyes at that moment set her heart racing and she wasn't going to tell him that Gavin had had a little too much to drink before he drove them home; not willingly at least. 'I didn't say——'

'You don't have to,' Campbell interrupted shortly, 'I saw enough from the window just now. Oh, I wasn't keeping an eye on whether or not he behaved himself, you don't have to protest; I heard the car and checked that it was you and not the cops, that's all.'

'It wasn't that serious,' she told him, thanking heaven she had resisted the temptation to kiss Gavin goodnight. She would have hated Campbell to draw the wrong conclusion from that.

'There was a new dent on the nearside wing,' he stated confidently, 'and knowing how, he coddles that old jalopy of his it won't have been there before he took you out. The paint was scraped off, and he'd never have neglected that.'

'You're very observant!' The retort was purely defensive, she realised, and hastily avoided his eyes. 'As a matter of fact we scraped the bank coming up the Deeside road.'

'Was he drunk?'

His mood troubled her and yet she did not quite know why, but it was the reason she hesitated to admit that Gavin had had more drink than was good for him. While she was considering whether or not to be frank about it, she put a hand to brush back the hair from her forehead and he noticed the bruise that had until then been hidden.

'You're hurt!' He came across the intervening few feet so quickly that she gasped when he lifted the hair from her forehead again and peered narrow-eyed at the bruise. 'Is this *all* you've got, or is there more?' His eyes burned with a ferocity she found hard to believe, and Chiara was shaking her head urgently at him. 'Good God,' he declared harshly, 'he takes you out to dinner and you come home looking as if he's beaten you up! What happened, Chiara?'

'Nothing happened!' She denied it breathlessly but didn't really expect him to believe it. 'Nothing as—as dramatic as you suggested anyway! It was as I said, we took a corner too fast——'

'*We?*'

'All right, *Gavin* misjudged a corner and we scraped the bank, that's all, and the car stalled. It took a while to get it going again and that's why I'm a bit later than I would normally have been, but it's no reason for you to—to go on like a Victorian father. There's no fear of *Gavin* grabbing me and kissing me whether I like it or not!'

It was a jibe she would have given anything to be able to recall, but it was too late and Campbell's eyes blazed at her for a moment, then were quickly concealed by lowered lids. His mouth was firm and set and just slightly crooked, although the smile was completely without humour, and she felt as if he had withdrawn from her suddenly.

'Campbell, I didn't mean——' She paused, biting anxiously on her lip. Her eyes were appealing, but it was doubtful if he would be moved by their appeal, though she tried to move him. 'I'm just a little drunk, I think,' she went on, 'and I didn't stop to think.'

'Why bother?' Campbell asked coolly. 'It's quite true; you're a hell of a lot safer with Gavin McDonald than you would have been with me, I've proved that often enough, haven't I? Incidentally,' he went on in the same cool voice, 'I wasn't waiting up for you with the intention of playing the heavy Victorian father, but to let you know that we had to call the doctor to Grandpa just after you left, which is probably why I over-reacted when you were later than I expected. You know the old saying—it never rains but it pours.'

'Grandpa?' Her own differences were forgotten, and she looked at him anxiously. 'Oh, Campbell, I'm sorry, I shouldn't have—— How serious is it? Is he very ill?'

'And tired,' Campbell said, and she realised suddenly how tired he looked himself. The small lines at the corners of his eyes and mouth were etched much more deeply than she had ever noticed before and it somehow heightened his likeness to their grandfather. 'The old boy is over eighty years old, Chiara, and he's—running down.'

'Oh, Cam!' She felt very small and ineffectual, knowing there was nothing she could do to put back the clock, but hating to think of Castle Eyrie without the grandfather she had only recently begun to really know and grow fond of. 'What—what can we do?'

'Nothing, little one.' His air of finality was frightening, and she wanted more than anything for him to forget that vow he had made and take her in his arms. She needed his kind of comfort almost desperately at the moment. 'It could be a few days or a few weeks,' he went on, as if he felt the hopelessness of the situation as hardly as she did. 'Grandpa was always a fighter, and he'll not give up easily, but this is something even he can't beat.'

So many emotions combined to overwhelm her and the sense of helplessness was perhaps stronger than any, for she did not know what to say or do next. Tears gathered in her eyes and there was nothing she could do to stop them. 'I—I wish I'd known him sooner,' she whispered, and it was purely instinct that made her turn to him when he opened his arms to her, folding her close as she buried her face against his shoulder. 'Campbell, I'm sorry, I'm truly sorry for what I said.'

He held her tightly, his face half-buried in silky black

hair, and neither of them said anything for quite some time, then he curved his long fingers about her cheek suddenly and lifted her face, looking down into it while she trembled in anticipation of his kiss. But instead of kissing her mouth he lightly brushed her forehead with his lips, and it was in such contrast to what showed in his eyes that Chiara caught her breath as he held her close again.

'No matter what the doc says,' he murmured with his mouth close to her ear, 'Grandpa says he's had no more than a wee bit upset, and he's got over them before, so why not now. He'd not like to know you were weeping over him, girl, so let's have no more tears, eh?' When he looked at her again it was with such infinite gentleness that it made his not having kissed her even harder to bear. 'As for you, my lass, I think you've had more than is good for you and you'd best go and sleep it off before you say anything else you'll be sorry for.'

'Cam——'

'Not Cam,' he reminded her in a half-whisper, and once again the hovering nearness of his mouth teased her senses almost unbearably. 'You know I don't like it. Now you away to your bed and get some sleep or you'll be fit for nothing in the morning!' He smiled at her with gleaming blue eyes that again stirred strange longings in her. 'We'll see what tomorrow brings, eh?'

'It was good of you to wait up for me,' she murmured, trying to match his seeming coolness. 'Thank you.'

There was nothing deliberate about the look she gave him from her huge dark eyes, nor was she aware of the soft sensuality of her mouth that almost smiled. 'Will you go to bed?' Campbell asked in a voice that slipped like a velvet glove along her spine. 'I've made a solemn promise never to touch you again, but if you go on looking at me with those eyes—— Have a heart, Chiara, go to bed!'

She laughed, because suddenly, despite the news he had just given concerning her grandfather and the very genuine sorrow she felt, there was a glowing warmth in her heart that she could not ignore. 'Goodnight, Campbell,' she whispered, and slipped out of the room, leaving him standing there with the overhead light burnishing his red-gold head. A big impressive man and one well worthy to be the next master of Castle Eyrie.

It did not strike her at that point that she was completely ignoring her own place in the scheme of things, for the Roberts had always held Castle Eyrie, and Campbell was a natural successor to their grandfather. Her own position could be determined later, and as yet she did not even hazard a guess at what it might be.

CHAPTER SEVEN

BECAUSE her grandfather's health was deteriorating so much more rapidly than any of them expected, the whole place was fraught with an atmosphere of sombre anticipation, and Chiara was reluctant to go anywhere for very long. She still lent a hand with the care of the animals, because whatever happened that could not be neglected, but she did so with less enthusiasm than before, and spent what time she could with her grandfather; a vigil she shared with the rest of the family.

There was nothing anyone could do, for he slept most of the time and his waking moments were almost more traumatic than sleep. His voice lacked its vigour and his eyes their canny brightness, and to Chiara the change was heartbreaking. She had become fond of her Grandfather Roberts and she felt for him with all the fervour of her Latin temperament, so that all else faded beside the sadness she felt at his diminishing awareness.

Only once had she met Gavin McDonald again, and that very briefly when she was in Roberts' Brae collecting fodder. An invitation to go out with him again, however, had been turned down because she felt she simply could not go anywhere and enjoy herself in the circumstances. He had been disappointed and made no secret of it, and at the back of her mind Chiara felt he did not entirely understand her state of mind.

In fact it was Campbell who eventually talked her into taking herself for a walk one day, and he was more persuasive. 'You need some fresh air, my girl,' he told her, and only the look in his eyes gave lie to his air of lightness. 'You've a face on you like a wee ghost, and you're no fit company for a man who needs cheerful faces about him. Away now,' he insisted when she looked like arguing. 'Go and check on old Yellow Nose for me.'

Unexpected support for the idea came from her aunt, although surely she needed rest and a change as much as anyone, and Chiara ventured to suggest as much. 'I'm older and less emotional,' Margaret Roberts insisted firmly, 'and you can do no good here, Chiara, you'd far better do as Campbell says and go for a walk.'

There had been a subtle difference in her aunt's manner during the past few days, and Chiara suspected that her devotion to her grandfather had been mostly responsible for it. Margaret was very fond of her father-in-law, whatever impression she gave to the contrary, and Chiara felt that her own loving care of the old man had perhaps given her a better insight into someone she had until then regarded as a foreign interloper and nothing more.

'If you're sure,' said Chiara, 'I won't be very long, Aunt Margaret.' It was automatic to glance at Campbell somehow and she did not realise quite how appealing the look was. 'I'll go and see what old Yellow Nose is up to, Campbell.'

'If only you could ride,' Campbell told her with obvious regret, 'you could have come with me, but I've to ride as far as the west ridge this morning and most of it is only accessible on horseback. Mebbe I'll see you on the way back, eh?'

It was as good as an invitation, Chiara felt, and she readily nodded acceptance of it. 'I don't suppose I'll get much further than the loch,' she said.

They left together and, because she felt she wanted to stay in his company as long as she could, Chiara walked round to the stable with him and was nothing loath to stop when he did, catching at her hand to delay her for a moment. His eyes scanned her pale face, and he shook his head slowly, regretfully, she felt. 'You *are* a pale and pasty wee creature,' he told her. 'We'll have to do something about it, Chiara; there's little use you making yourself ill, and it's the last thing Grandpa would want, you must know that.'

His concern touched her as it always did, and she managed a faint smile as she looked up, noting the dark smudges below his own eyes. 'What about you?' she asked, and reached up to lightly draw a fingertip around under his left eye. 'You've got dark smudges under your eyes too.'

'Bad for my image, do you think?' he teased, but his quizzical expression did not reach his eyes which still looked darker and sadder than she had ever seen them, and affected her quite alarmingly. He glanced briefly at his wrist-watch and shook his head with obvious regret. 'I just wish you could ride with me, lass, but I have to get on; just mind and don't overdo it, eh?'

She nodded agreement and her heart beat much harder and faster when he half turned to go, then turned back. But he seemed to think better of whatever he had had in mind and, because she had been anticipating his kiss, her disappointment showed in her eyes for a moment before she hastily concealed them. As she watched him ride off a few minutes later she regretted yet again not having taken him up on his offer to teach her to ride.

Nevertheless walking proved relaxing and she was warm and glowing in no time at all, so that when she reached the loch she stood for several minutes and allowed her hair to be tossed and tumbled by the brisk breeze. There was something very special about this vast open countryside that she was more and more beginning to look on as her own, and she was in no hurry to turn back now that she was there, for its air of peace was infectious.

Recalling the ostensible reason for her being there, she

scanned the hot summer sky for some sign of the eagle, but saw nothing of it. What she did see, however, as she stood with one hand shading her eyes, was a vehicle in the distance, over where Gavin McDonald grazed his sheep, and she recognised it as his old jeep.

It wasn't so far away that he might not see her if she waved a hand, for the light was clear and sharp, and out on the moors it was often possible to see incredible distances. Acting purely on instinct, she raised a hand and waved, although she was not really surprised when he didn't respond, for in all probability he hadn't noticed her beside the vastness of the loch.

But the jeep turned suddenly and splashed through the burn, spray sparkling in the sunlight as he crossed the natural boundary between the two properties. It was a completely unexpected turn of events to see it come bumping and bouncing over the tussocky heather towards her, and Chiara watched it curiously and a little doubtfully, wondering what on earth had got into Gavin to make him act with such unaccustomed boldness.

One of the things that Campbell had more than once commented on was Gavin's lack of push, and as he came closer she wondered what Campbell would have said to this latest development. Knowing something of how he felt, she thanked heaven that for the moment Campbell was safely over on the west ridge.

Flushed and for once bareheaded, Gavin drove the jeep right up beside her before he stopped, and there was a kind of defensive look in his eyes as he got out, brushing his hands in an obviously nervous gesture down his shirt. 'I thought I'd come over and see you,' he said, dispensing with any kind of greeting. 'How are you, Chiara? How is your grandfather?'

He had the musty smell of woollies about him and his brow and upper lip were beaded with perspiration which he brushed at with a forearm while he waited for her response. In this situation he seemed almost as frankly earthy as Campbell did, but he lacked Campbell's confidence, and that won Chiara's sympathy.

'I'm fine, thank you, Gavin.' She eased her shoulders in a helpless shrug over her grandfather's condition because it wasn't a subject she could easily discuss without becoming emotional, and somehow she did not see Gavin McDonald as a man who either showed or understood emotion. 'Grandpa—there's really nothing we can do; he simply gets weaker every day.'

'Aye well,' Gavin observed matter-of-factly, 'he'll be a very old man now, will he not? Over eighty years old, it is not so surprising, Chiara.' He went on, and his voice did not noticeably change from its cool matter-of-factness. 'And is it Colin Roberts will soon be the new laird, then?'

It struck a harsh note, that cool mention of her grandfather's successor, and it was very hard to accept in her present mood, and yet she knew that to tenants like Gavin the identity of the new laird was of some importance. So much could depend on the new landlord's policy, and it was common knowledge that Colin was less in favour of the reserve than either his son or his father. It would suit Gavin to think that the next in line for Castle Eyrie would perhaps do something about the wild life that caused him so much concern.

Chiara, however, had no intention of letting him know that her grandfather was not following tradition and leaving it to his son, and she once again shrugged her dislike of the question. 'That remains to be seen,' she told him, but somehow got the feeling that it was exactly the answer he expected, for he nodded briefly.

'Oh yes, to be sure,' he agreed.

'I'm sorry, Gavin, but I can't talk about it——'

'But of course you cannot! I shouldn't have asked when you're feeling as you do.' He was seemingly at a

loss for a moment, and in her present state of mind
Chiara did not ease the way for him as she might normally have done. 'You look very pale and tired,' he said
after several moments, and she smiled ruefully.

'No more than anyone else,' she told him. 'It's a very
—traumatic time for all of us, watching Grandpa——'
She swallowed hard but went on when she was able to.
'With someone so desperately ill and just—waiting all
the time, we're all tired and edgy.'

'Aye, you will be.' He reached for her hand and held
it tightly for a moment and his eyes, she noticed, did not
quite meet hers. 'I'm glad you called me over, Chiara,
for I've been wanting to see you again.'

'Oh, but all I did was wave my hand,' Chiara told
him, hastily correcting any false impression. 'I didn't
even know it was possible to drive across the burn.'

'It is at that point,' said Gavin, and clearly he was not
discouraged because he squeezed the fingers he held and
looked, if possible, more earnest than ever. 'And you'll
not send me packing now that I'm here, will you,
Chiara?'

She smiled faintly, thinking it would take a harder
heart than hers to send him packing, for there was something very appealing about his air of dour solemnity
somehow. 'No, of course I won't do that,' she promised,
and the hand holding hers tightened its hold just a fraction.

'Chiara—Chiara, I've never met a woman like you
before, and you will mebbe think I'm too—pushy, not
having known you for very long, but I have to say this.
I could get—I have already got, very fond of you; very
fond indeed, Chiara, do you take my meaning?'

Chiara took his meaning quite clearly, and she wished
with all her heart that she had resisted the impulse to
wave a friendly greeting, for this wasn't the sort of
situation she wanted to have to cope with at the moment.

'I think I understand, Gavin,' she said, and found it very hard to face that earnest and slightly anxious look without feeling strangely guilty somehow.

'You're a very lovely girl,' he went on, stumbling a little in his anxiety and flushing as pink as a schoolboy. 'I never saw anyone lovelier in my life, and you've —affected me in a way that no one ever has before. I know it's a very short time since we first met, Chiara, and I mebbe don't know you as well as I could, but— Och, what I'm trying to say is that I'm altogether *too* fond of you!'

She wanted to stop him before he went any further, but Chiara found it harder than she would have believed. 'Gavin, I know what you're trying to say, and——'

'You do not!' Gavin denied vehemently, and she noticed a fine film of moisture beading his upper lip as he gazed at her with those earnest eyes. 'Mebbe you're accustomed to men telling you that they've fallen in love with you at first sight, but it's not a thing I've ever believed was possible until now. I find it hard to believe it's happened even now, but it's true, Chiara, I love you and I want to marry you!'

After a few meetings, most of them brief and some of them not exactly amicable, Chiara thought it unlikely that he was in love, flattering as it would be to believe it, but she couldn't doubt he felt something for her, for only a genuine belief in what he was saying would drive a man like Gavin McDonald to make such a claim as he had just made. How to cope with the situation was something beyond her scope at the moment, and Chiara felt her heart hammering hard and bringing a warm flush to her own cheeks as she took a moment to recover.

'Gavin——'

'You like me well enough, do you not?' he insisted, and she could not in all honesty deny that, so she nodded.

'And I'm not a—a man for the women,' he went on, leaving Chiara in little doubt who he was alluding to. 'I'd make a good husband, Chiara, I promise you that.'

It was much too hard to simply come right out with it and tell him that she just didn't think of him in that light at all; not as a husband. 'I'm sure you would, Gavin, but I can't believe—I mean, you said yourself that we've known each other such a very short time, and you should be more sure first.'

'I'm sure enough!'

Chiara's hands expressed her helplessness. She had never seen such a look in Gavin's eyes before and the gleaming determination of it alarmed her. 'It's only two months, Gavin, only *just* two months, not long enough to be in love.'

'You'll not convince me otherwise!' he warned in that sober, unsmiling way of his, and Chiara had to believe he meant it.

'I'm—very flattered,' she murmured, not knowing what to say or do at the moment.

'I've never met a woman like you before,' he went on in a voice that was perceptibly rougher and less controlled. 'I want to marry you, Chiara! I'm asking you to marry me!'

Again she tried to find some way of saying what she had to say without being cruelly frank and unfeeling, but still she couldn't summon the right words. His earnestness and the anxious look in his eyes made her a coward about saying the wrong thing, and she had had no forewarning of the situation.

But before she could say a word he had reached out and pulled her into his arms, taking her completely by surprise and startling her with his clumsiness. He held her in a steely grip that she had little hope of escaping, but he sought her mouth with such a lack of finesse that he was obviously much less practised than Campbell was.

To struggle was instinctive, just as it was instinctive to compare him with Campbell, and quite automatic. The more she struggled the more determinedly he held her, and she was breathing hard, almost past struggling, when she caught sight of something from the corner of her eye that renewed her determination to shake him off.

'No, Gavin!'

Turning her head, she thrust her hands against him in a desperate effort to be free, and eventually he let her go with obvious reluctance. But his eyes still burned with a gleaming fierceness and his breathing was short and rapidly uneven.

Once free, Chiara confirmed what she had only glimpsed at before, and she sighed inwardly at the sight of Campbell veering off suddenly and riding as fast as he could drive the hard-breathing stallion, in the direction of Castle Eyrie. Of course he had seen what was happening, and yet he had simply turned away, and she hated to think what interpretation he had put on what he had seen.

Capable at last of realising something beside his own emotional desires, Gavin followed the direction of her gaze, and perhaps for a moment he showed a trace of uncertainty. But it was obvious that in the long run he was less troubled by the idea of them having been observed than Chiara was.

'What happens now?' he asked, and Chiara turned and looked at him.

Condemnation for his thoughtlessness trembled on her tongue for a moment, but then she recalled that Campbell, by his own admission, had forsworn his claim to her, and she shrugged wryly as she turned once more to follow the progress of man and horse across the wide moor. 'What should happen?' she countered a little breathlessly. 'Campbell doesn't own me!'

'Does he know that?'

The hint of malice was unmistakable, and she flushed

as she turned again to watch the departing rider riding hard towards the castle. There was something about the angle of his head and the firm straightness of his back that suggested he was angry, and the possible cause of his anger fluttered little chills along her spine.

'He does now,' she murmured, and withdrew her hand from Gavin's anxiously seeking one, automatically.

'Do you mind?' he demanded, and his voice had that edge of harshness again so that she took a moment or two to reply.

'I mind anyone—whoever it is getting the wrong idea about what just happened,' she told him, and her voice quavered slightly.

'The wrong idea?' Gavin insisted, and she supposed it could have been more tactfully worded if she had stopped to think.

'I'm sorry, Gavin——' She shrugged ruefully and shook her head. 'I really ought to go back; I've been gone quite a long time and I promised Aunt Margaret I wouldn't be too long.'

But Gavin reached for her hands again, seemingly determined to know where he stood. 'And what about me, Chiara?' he pressed. 'Will you marry me?'

There was no other course for her but to be frank with him, she realised, but she hoped he was going to understand and not consider her too unfeeling. 'Gavin, at the moment, with things as they are with Grandpa, I just— I'm sorry.'

'But you'll not turn me down altogether?'

She had made a mistake, using her grandfather to qualify her refusal, she realised, but she was anxious to escape the situation and she sought an easy way out. 'I —I like you, Gavin.'

'Then when things are easier for you, you'll consider me?' he urged, and he had never looked more earnest and appealing. 'Promise me, Chiara!'

It was an easy way out and she had too much on her mind at the moment to cope with another proposal of marriage, however different in character it was from Campbell's unorthodox one. So she sighed and attempted a smile that did not quite reach her eyes, hoping that she was not going to live to regret her faintheartedness.

'I promise I'll think about it,' she told him.

'And—will you tell Campbell Roberts about it?'

She felt her heart lurch sickeningly for a moment and she looked at him warily. 'There's nothing to tell anyone,' she insisted in as cool a voice as she could muster in the circumstances, and the speculative look in his eyes fell before her own questioning one.

'No, no, to be sure.'

The castle and its hill loomed over the advancing rider for a few moments before he disappeared below the ramparts of towering rock, and Chiara had the most curious feeling suddenly that the sun had gone in and there was less warmth in the air. 'I'd better go,' she said, and turned to make her own, slower way back, glancing back only for a second. 'Goodbye, Gavin.'

Campbell had said nothing so far about seeing her with Gavin, and it was almost a week now, so that he would surely have made some mention of it if he intended doing so. He had been quiet, almost morose, at times, but that could be accounted for by the same situation that made the entire household more sombre, for old Ian Roberts was slipping fast into oblivion.

At times it seemed that he had already gone, for the vital spark that had made him the man he was had already been dimmed, and there seemed no similarity between the frail shell who hung between life and death, and the lusty old man who had ruled autocratically but lovingly over his family for so long.

Chiara would miss him as much as the rest of his

family would, but she was young and the oppressive atmosphere of anticipation touched her differently. It was as a relief from the gloom of the sickroom that she found her way down to the stable with nothing particular in mind except some vague idea of looking at the wildcat that still fascinated her.

Its thin little body had fattened out in captivity, but its ferocity was undiminished, and as she crouched down beside its box, Chiara scolded it softly. 'You ungrateful creature, you don't deserve to be fed and coddled as you are!'

She reached for its empty food dish, but snatched her arm back quickly to avoid a swiftly aimed paw with claws extended. The rolled back sleeve of her jacket caught on the wire catch of the pen and when she snatched back the knitted wool pulled the catch open, allowing the crudely made door to swing open. Already prowling in the wire run that had been constructed to accommodate its increasing activity, the wildcat saw its chance with the unerring instinct of wild creatures for freedom.

In a split second it had slipped quickly through the open door and was streaking for the sunlight outside, its ears flat and its boldly striped fur bristling a challenge to anyone who might think of trying to stop it. Chiara was fully aware of her limitations, but she was mindful of the outcome when one of the wolves had escaped and been shot, so she dived forward unthinkingly, missing it by inches.

Out into the yard the creature went, only to come face to face with the old stable cat, a piebald moggy of advanced years who had always been suspicious of the newcomer. Seeing the domestic cat apparently set on a confrontation, Chiara yelled out at it, trying to avert disaster, for the wildcat would brook no interference now.

'No, Thomas, stop it!'

Her warning went unheeded, so she bent and picked up the yard cat, but its back was arched and it was bent on fighting; deprived of its chosen antagonist, it lashed out furiously and caught Chiara's forearm, scoring a long angry slash in the soft flesh. Dropping him swiftly, she cursed him in Italian while her eyes followed the wildcat as it disappeared out through the yard gate and to freedom.

She was still standing with one hand holding her scratched arm when Campbell came up behind her, his firm tread ominous and unmistakable on the cobbles. Always a believer in taking the initiative when she had inadvertently done something that called for explanation, she spoke up quickly before he even reached her.

'Campbell, I'm sorry, but the wildcat's gone. I didn't let it out on purpose, but my sleeve caught on the catch and the minute the door was open she was away before I could stop her.'

'I hope you *didn't* try to stop her,' he said shortly, and pointed to the arm she held. 'Did it scratch you?'

'No, it was——'

'Let me see!' He took her arm and examined the damage, his long fingers hurting almost as much as the scratch did. 'I suppose you were trying to stroke the damned thing,' he guessed unsympathetically, and Chiara flushed at the inevitability of it.

'I told you what happened,' she reminded him.

'So you did!' The blue eyes gleamed at her from below thick brown lashes and she knew then just how much he had disliked seeing Gavin McDonald kissing her. 'Maybe you're working in league with your farmer boy-friend to let loose my stock one by one?'

The look she gave him was enough to convey how she felt, and for some reason she could not understand, it was a kind of satisfaction she felt at his obvious dislike, rather than anger. 'You know better than that,' she told him.

'And it wasn't the wildcat that scratched me, it was Thomas when I tried to stop him fighting with it.'

He examined her arm more closely, frowning over it as if it was worse than he expected, and in fact it was quite a deep score that stung painfully and oozed blood in a thin red line down her forearm. Campbell huffed his dissatisfaction, then turned, still holding her arm, and started back across the yard.

Stumbling after him on the uneven cobbles, Chiara protested, 'Don't go so fast, your legs are longer than mine and I can't keep up!'

'Then run!' he instructed callously, and Chiara's voice rose indignantly.

'Campbell!'

She was breathing hard, but it was not only breathlessness that accounted for the flush in her cheeks, it was the burning harshness that showed in his eyes and in the way he held her. He surely could not believe she was in league with Gavin McDonald against him, and yet she could trace his determined disregard of her only from that unexpected kiss of Gavin's that he had witnessed.

She came to a halt in the middle of the yard and snatched her arm free, wincing as she did so, but facing him with bright reproachful eyes. 'You've been trying to think of some way of—of getting back at me ever since you saw me talking to Gavin the other day,' she accused huskily, and he continued to regard her with the same steely scrutiny until she felt like screaming at him in sheer frustration.

'You've a better grasp of the vernacular than I gave you credit for,' he told her, repeating the phrase she had used. 'Getting back at me—what kind of English is that?'

'The same kind that you use!' Chiara retorted. 'And you know perfectly well what I mean, Campbell!'

'I know,' he agreed. 'Just as I know you were not

simply talking with Gavin McDonald the other day!'

'He—he kissed me——'

'I know that, I saw him kissing you, though he wasn't making a very good job of it from what I could see! But then I suppose you make allowances as he's not had my experience!' His vivid blue eyes were gleaming as she had not seen them do for some time, and she was almost glad to have angered him if only because it banished that deep sad look that had haunted his eyes lately. 'He has the nerve of the devil,' he went on, his big hands back-turned on his hips while he glared at her. 'Not only sneaking over on to our property to see you, but making himself very much at home, from all I saw!'

'He didn't sneak over,' Chiara denied automatically, and he gathered his brows into a frown.

'You invited him?'

Her blood pounded in the old familiar way as she met that challenging look, though she had no intention of leaving him with the impression that she had asked Gavin to come over. 'Not exactly,' she demurred. 'But I waved my hand when I saw him and he came over; I didn't realise it was possible to cross the burn at that point.'

'But he wasn't unwelcome, obviously!'

'I *like* Gavin!' He stood watching her, waiting to hear her admit to something more than liking, and she moistened her lips anxiously. 'I—well, I admit that it took me by surprise when he kissed me.'

'I don't see why it should,' Campbell observed more softly. 'He's a man, for all he's as dour as a kirk elder!'

She flicked her gaze evasively. 'It just didn't seem like him to do it, somehow, but——' She glanced up at him again, and tried to judge his reaction before she went on. 'He—Gavin says he's in love with me.'

She wasn't sure what she had hoped to achieve by telling him, but his vehemence was unexpected. '*Does* he, by God!'

'You don't believe it?' she challenged, but Campbell was shaking his head.

'Oh, I can see it's possible,' he allowed with unexpected quietness, 'but it's a mighty hasty move for a man who studies every move as carefully as Gavin McDonald normally does.' The touch of his hand on her cheek was as unexpected as Gavin's kiss had been and much more disturbing. 'You've not done anything foolish, have you, girl?' he asked, and it was concern she recognised in his voice, she felt sure, not jealousy.

'I—I haven't committed myself to anything, if that's what you mean,' she told him, and looked at the top button of his shirt rather than directly at him. 'I told him that I couldn't think about anything for the moment while Grandpa was so ill.' He flicked a brief glance upward. 'He asked me to marry him.'

'*Damn* the man for his cheek!' Campbell exploded fiercely, and once more his ferocity startled her.

'Because he's asked me to marry him?' Chiara asked, and the look in her eyes challenged him in a way he couldn't mistake. '*You* did, and it wasn't because you loved me!' She held his gaze for as long as she was able, then went on in a small and slightly breathless voice, 'Or maybe you're just angry because he dared set foot on what you're pleased to call your property!'

Campbell reached and stroked a hand over the dark silky softness of her hair for a moment, then he grasped it hard suddenly, making her gasp and tipping back her head, his eyes glowing as he towered over her. 'Or maybe I think it amounts to the same thing,' he murmured in a quiet, shiver-inducing voice, and pulled back her head still further while he looked down at her mouth, eager and trembling, and waiting for his kiss. 'Don't push me too far, you black-eyed brat,' he whispered, then laughed shortly and let her go. Taking her arm instead and leading her once more across the yard, 'Let's put something on that arm before it turns nasty; I don't want you going down with blood-poisoning.'

In fact it was only a couple of days later that her arm did begin to show signs of being infected, and although it was less serious than blood-poisoning the result was both painful and unpleasant, and it was the considered opinion of the doctor that she should give up working with the animals for the time being.

Campbell had driven her down to Roberts' Brae for the necessary injection, and they were mounting the steps on their return, when the door opened and her uncle stood in the doorway. Campbell took one look at his father's expression then glanced past him, Colin shaking his head slowly. 'A few minutes ago,' he said, and neither of them needed to mention what had happened in their absence.

Campbell's open, outdoor face seemed to have become closed suddenly, and his mouth had a firm straight look that at least served to keep it steady. Chiara was less able to control hers, and it quivered warningly so that she caught her bottom lip between her teeth. Campbell's hand under her arm was withdrawn and she felt doubly bereft when he walked past his father and made for the stairs.

'Take care of Chiara for me,' he said in a flat deep voice, and seemed to see nothing out of place in speaking as he did. 'Be gentle, Father, and don't let her come upstairs—not yet.'

Her uncle nodded, accepting both his instruction and his right to give it. Colin took her arm and led her across the hall to the big sitting-room, but for as long as she could Chiara watched Campbell taking the stairs two at a time with his long legs. She felt numb and yet at the same time strangely relieved, for the threat of it had hung over them for so long that it was hard to see the end as anything but another inevitable step on the downward path.

A curious kind of quiet seemed to have fallen, and only in the privacy of her own room some time later did Chiara weep as fulsomely as her emotional nature required her to. The old castle had seen so many generations of Roberts come and go and the departure of old Ian was merely the end of another chapter in its history, but she would miss him.

Most hard hit was Margaret, his daughter-in-law, and she seemed almost to crumble. Chiara found it hard to believe that such a stern, unyielding woman could weep so bitterly and heartbrokenly over anyone, but the last weeks had taken their toll of even her strong will. Also she had genuinely loved the old man into whose family she had been more or less forced to marry and, perhaps more than either her husband or her son could, Chiara understood the kind of love-hate relationship she had had with the old man. Because in some ways it resembled her own relationship with Campbell.

Campbell simply carried on as usual, and it was probably his way of containing his grief, for he had been very close to his grandfather; much closer than she had been herself, Chiara realised. It was unlikely that becoming the new laird would make much difference to his lifestyle either, for he was totally committed to what he was doing.

Chiara for her part could not help wondering if Gavin McDonald, and possibly others as well, were banking on Colin inheriting and perhaps running down the reserve, for it was well known that her uncle was less than interested and was unlikely to expend a large percentage of the estate's income on the project. It was because it was on her mind that she mentioned it to her uncle the day following her grandfather's death, while they sat talking together and feeling somewhat at a loss.

'Learning that Campbell and I are to have Castle Eyrie between us is going to come as a shock to a lot of people,' she suggested. 'I still find it hard to accept myself, that Grandpa left you out and gave it to us, and most people are going to find it hard to believe.'

They had the big sitting-room to themselves at the moment, and Colin seemed more relaxed than he had for some time; possibly because the strain of his father's illness was at last over. When he looked across at her, his expression was faintly quizzical. 'I think you'll find it's been suspected for some time,' he told her. 'There isn't much that goes on in a place like this that doesn't soon become common knowledge, although one does sometimes wonder how it happens and what starts the rumour. I heard about it myself some weeks ago, and I gathered it was pretty common knowledge by then.'

To Chiara it was scarcely believable. 'Do you mean that people actually knew about it?' she asked, seeing an implication far deeper than anything her uncle did, and he shook his head.

'I don't say they knew, my dear, but a lot of them had a very good idea of what Father had planned for the estate, and certainly most of our tenants did. It was old Hamish Grieve who asked me outright, he has more nerve than Gavin McDonald, though I don't doubt he was just as anxious to have it confirmed or no.'

Chiara's heart was beating hard and she had never in her life hoped so fervently to be wrong. 'When was this, Uncle Colin? How long ago?'

Her curiosity and her obvious anxiety puzzled him, but he gave her as accurate a reply as he was able to. 'It would be about two—maybe three weeks ago, I suppose. They'd obviously been discussing it, but old Hamish came right out with it and asked me; not that I satisfied his curiosity, of course.'

Before Gavin had made that uncharacteristically impulsive offer of marriage, Chiara realised, and coped for a moment or two with the bitter truth of it. She would have liked to think that one proposal of marriage at least had been made without the motive of avarice, but it seemed she had taken a too innocent view of Gavin's professed love for her.

'It seems a bit much when private family business is known and discussed by all and sundry,' she declared, with such bitterness that her uncle looked at her curiously.

'Oh, it isn't as serious as all that, my dear,' he told her. 'It was probably arrived at simply by putting two and two together; you and Cam have been working together on the project and it wouldn't be hard for someone to come to the conclusion that you would eventually come into the estate. It's well known, too, that I'm far more interested in the distillery than in the castle estate.' He smiled at her reassuringly. 'The Highland grapevine has been a pretty reliable source of information, and speculation, for centuries, and it's amazing how right it is sometimes.'

Seeing Gavin leaving the little family chapel the following day, Chiara recalled with resentment his apparent foreknowledge of old Ian's will and his subsequent attempt to get her to marry him. For she could no longer believe that it had been prompted by love of her. It was no surprise to see him visiting the chapel, for during the next few days most of the estate workers and some of the villagers would be coming to pay their respects to the old laird, and Gavin would never be remiss in matters of that kind.

If she could have avoided contact with him Chiara would have done, but it was too late once he had seen her and started his approach. He carried his hat, and a black band around one sleeve marked his respect for her grandfather; the grave expression was normal to him, but in keeping with the occasion, and he had his eyes on her long before he got within speaking distance.

Once he was face to face with her, however, his gaze became evasive, though he was properly polite and only a little less than formal. 'It will be a sad time for you, Chiara,' he said in his soft, precise accent. 'May I say how sorry I am.'

'It was only to be expected, as you pointed out to me,' she reminded him huskily, and plainly he sensed something that made him uneasy, for he drew his brows anxiously.

'Will you be doing anything to change that—menagerie now that you are a partner in the estate?' he asked, and Chiara felt her heart thud in protest.

She felt a flash of anger at his frankly expressed interest at such a moment and did little to disguise it. 'You know,' she accused, and Gavin replied quickly, defensively, she realised; without stopping to think.

'It has been rumoured in the village for weeks, Chiara!'

Quite clearly at the moment he did not consider how much he had given away, and Chiara tried to quell her bitterness in vain. 'So I understand,' she told him. 'The Highland grapevine is a very reliable means of gathering information, so I've been told, but I didn't realise you knew I was to share Castle Eyrie with Campbell, Gavin!'

'Not to say I *know*,' Gavin quibbled cautiously. 'I have only heard the rumour as others have heard it, Chiara.'

'Before you made that—that dramatic declaration of love and asked me to marry you!' Chiara accused, and saw realisation dawn at last.

He cast a half-hidden, wary glance over her face, then shook his head slowly. 'I still feel about you as I did, whether or not you have Castle Eyrie,' he insisted. 'It makes no difference to the way I feel, Chiara.'

But it made a difference to her, and as she stood in the shade of the rowans that decked the sombre little churchyard with bright red berries, Chiara thought how much more honest Campbell had been with his bold and frankly mercenary proposal. She had been right now to believe Gavin McDonald an emotional and impulsive lover, and she knew now why he had acted so out of character. It was a bitter pill to have to swallow all over again and as she faced him a chill fluttered along her spine.

She just wanted to escape that evasive and vaguely apologetic gaze before she said something she would be sorry for, and she shook her head. 'I have to go,' she whispered in a voice that shook alarmingly. 'I—I promised Aunt Margaret I'd be straight back, there's so much to be done.' It seemed quite illogical to wish that Campbell could have been there to lend his support. 'Please excuse me.'

'Chiara!' She turned back to face him only very unwillingly, and she snatched away her hands when he would have taken them in his. His eyes were dark and perhaps regretful, she was in no mood to recognise any regret but her own. 'I'm sorry,' he said, and she acknowledged the apology without speaking, for she was suddenly bereft of things to say.

'Goodbye,' she said huskily, and turned and left him.

CHAPTER EIGHT

CHIARA had told herself more than once that there was nothing deliberate in the fact that she had seen nothing more of Gavin McDonald during the nearly three months since her grandfather died, it had just happened that way. But she was thankful for it just the same. Being unable to drive the Land Rover for a while because of a painful arm had been partly responsible, for there had been fewer opportunities of meeting him by accident in the village, and he was unlikely to ever have the nerve to come and see her at home, after that last difficult occasion.

Her inactivity had achieved one good thing, however, in that she now had a much closer relationship with her aunt, something she would have found hard to believe at one time. The change had begun while her grandfather was ill, and progressed during the enforced inactivity. Not that Margaret's feelings had changed concerning her sharing Castle Eyrie with Campbell, but at least she was not now regarded as simply a foreign intruder and nothing else, and the atmosphere was much more congenial.

October was a mild month, and that, with the changing colours on the moors, frequently lured Chiara out for long walks when she was not busy. The part she played in helping to run Castle Eyrie was increasingly important, and indeed Murdoch had assured her that she was not only a very welcome addition, but a very useful one too.

Campbell was noncommittal on the same subject, but he was much less inclined to treat her as a complete ignoramus, although her relationship with him remained in a very unsatisfactory state of limbo. Nothing had changed one way or the other, and she sometimes felt unaccountably restless and impatient.

As things stood, neither of them could claim legal ownership of the estate until their grandfather's will had been through probate, and that seemed to be taking an interminable time, adding to Chiara's sense of uncertainty. It did not even occur to her to return to Italy for good, for she seemed to have found her niche at Castle Eyrie, and although she missed the sunnier clime of her native Tuscany, she was enough her mother's daughter to love Scotland too.

It was while she was returning from Houstons' farm one morning with a load of hay that she came into collision with a large American car. It had been coming from the opposite direction, and she wasn't quite sure who was most to blame in fact. The other driver had been on the wrong side of the road, certainly, but, perhaps with the familiarity that breeds contempt, she had been too near the centre of the road.

Fortunately neither vehicle had been going very fast and the clash was a very minor one, but just for a moment or two all the breath had been knocked out of Chiara and it took her several moments to recover as she slumped over the wheel. She stirred only when an anxious male voice brought her back to reality; a voice that spoke with what she recognised as a local accent overlaid with a hint of Transatlantic.

'I'm sorry,' it said, and a car door closing suggested the driver was concerned enough to have got out and come back to check on the damage. 'Oh, my God,' it went on when she did not move, 'what have I done!'

Whoever he was, Chiara couldn't hold him entirely to blame, and she raised her head at last and shook it slowly in an attempt to clear it. Her side ached and she felt a bit dazed, but there was no real harm done, and she even managed a faint smile when the man bent over her solicitously. He was a very large man, she noted, with light blue eyes that looked down at her anxiously, while he rested a large hand on her shoulder.

'Are you O.K.?'

Chiara nodded. 'I'm O.K. Just winded.'

Breathing deeply enough to speak made her ache worse so that she rather illogically wished that she need not breathe for a few minutes until it passed. 'Can you move?' he enquired, and again she nodded, sitting upright behind the wheel and concentrating on taking only shallow breaths. 'Take it easy,' the man advised. 'I'll get a doctor to look at you. Unless,' he added hopefully, 'you can walk that far, can you?'

'Yes, I think so; but I don't need a doctor, I'm perfectly O.K.'

'Better safe than sorry,' he quoted, and opened the door of the Land Rover so that she could swing her legs out.

Even in a village as small as Roberts' Brae it was possible to collect onlookers, and Chiara wondered how long it would be before the local constable put in an appearance. Then the group of onlookers parted and stepped back, as if someone had cut a swathe through them, and Gavin McDonald came through, thrusting with his elbows and wearing a grim air of purpose.

He came to a halt in front of her, ignoring the stranger for the moment and wearing a frown as black as thunder. 'Chiara, what on earth has happened to you? Are you all right?'

'I guess it was my fault,' the big man told him. 'I was on the wrong side of the road and I didn't see the lady.' Chiara intended to distribute the blame more evenly, but before she could say anything he apparently recognised Gavin and took a moment to greet him. 'Hey, Gavin! Hello!'

Gavin's recognition of him was chilling to say the

least, but he was never a very effusive man and he was
probably too concerned about Chiara at the moment to
trouble himself with anything else. He gave the man a
brief nod of recognition, then took both Chiara's hands
in his and gazed anxiously into her pale face.

'I'll get Doctor Massie,' he told her, taking charge
unhesitatingly. 'And you'd best not move until he's
seen you, Chiara.'

Making a big issue out of a very minor incident was
the last thing she wanted, and especially since she suspected Gavin of trying to do just that for his own purpose, and she would have objected yet again to the
doctor being called. In the meantime, however, the
doctor had emerged from his house only a few yards
further down the hill, and a few brusque words were
enough to send most of the onlookers about their business.

Only Gavin and the big redhaired man remained
while the doctor made a cursory check on the spot, and
Chiara noticed how warily the two of them eyed one
another. It was Gavin who eventually took the initiative again, though he gave the man no name, and he
still had not returned his initial greeting.

'You have no need to wait,' he told him. 'I'll stay with
Miss Manti and see that she's all right. You will very
probably be hearing from Charlie Houston,' he added,
and the malice in the words was unmistakable. Nor did
Chiara believe it was entirely on her account.

'I was just as much to blame, Gavin,' she told him
swiftly, and the doctor looked up for a moment and
caught her eye.

'You're O.K. apart from a few bruises,' he assured
her, and lowered one lid in a suggestion of wink as he
added, 'And what Charlie Houston doesn't know won't
hurt him, eh, Miss Manti? I'll help you along to the
surgery and put something on your bruises, then ring

Campbell and tell him to come and fetch you. Better not try driving again just yet.'

'Oh, but I'm perfectly able to drive,' Chiara insisted, but the doctor eyed her soberly.

'Would you have me risk Campbell's wrath by letting you drive yourself home?' he demanded. 'No, my dear, far better to let him come and fetch you. By the time he gets here you'll probably feel as if you've been run over by a bus and be glad of a chauffeur.'

It was probably true, but Chiara's rueful face anticipated Campbell's reaction. 'I'm not going to be very popular, putting myself out of action again.'

'There's no need to get Campbell out,' Gavin interrupted before the doctor could reply. 'I can take you home, Chiara.'

It was up to her, Chiara realised, and the doctor was eyeing her with undisguised speculation while he helped her from the car. At the moment she wasn't overly concerned with Gavin's feelings, but she was quite sure she didn't want a confrontation between him and Campbell at the moment, so she shook her head at him.

'I'd rather Campbell came for me, thank you, Gavin,' she told him. 'He can bring Murdoch with him to drive the Land Rover back.'

For a moment it looked as if he might argue, but then he shrugged and thrust both hands into his pockets, his mouth down-turned and a reproachful look in his eyes. All of which the redhaired man noted with some interest. 'Will I see you again?' he asked, and she paused for a moment, with the doctor holding her arm and the redhaired man watching curiously.

'It's possible,' she told him, studiously offhand. 'Thank you, Gavin—goodbye.'

Despite her determination, her soft heart was touched by the sombre look of reproach he gave her before he turned away, and when she looked back just a few

moments later she saw that he was in conversation with
the redhaired man. Just before she stepped inside the
doctor's front door she noticed him getting into the big
American car, so presumably they knew one another
fairly well after all.

Campbell had promised the doctor he would see that
she took things easy for a few days, but Chiara saw no
harm in taking it easy outside instead. The sun was
shining and it was quite mild, mild enough for her to
roll up the sleeves of her jacket as she sat on a bale of
hay out in the yard.

It was sheltered there and there was a certain air of
privacy about the enclosed yard that she liked, and a
bale of hay was as comfortable as any armchair as she
sat playing with the stable cat. It was there that Campbell found her, and he heaved a sigh of exasperation
as he came across the yard, his booted feet thudding
ominously.

'You are a ruddy little menace,' he informed her without apparent rancour, and she glanced up at him through
her lashes while she stroked a purring Thomas curled
up beside her. 'Did I not promise the doc I'd look after
you for the next day or two?' he demanded, and stood
in front of her with his hands on his hips in that unconsciously arrogant stance he sometimes affected. 'Is
it too much to ask that you find somewhere more suitable to recover than a pile of hay in the stable yard?'

'I'm all right,' she assured him, keeping her eyes on
the cat. 'It's warm and I like being outside.'

'You like being cussed!' Campbell retorted. 'You're
always getting into something and needing to be rescued!'

'You didn't *have* to rescue me in this instance,' Chiara
told him pertly. 'Gavin had already offered to drive me
home!'

His eyes watched her so intently that she was almost

forced to look up at him sooner or later. 'I gather you turned him down, as Doctor Massie asked me to come for you?' he said.

'Obviously!'

He didn't follow it up as she half expected him to, but reached for the arm that still showed a very faint pink mark down its soft inner skin. 'And I'd have thought you would choose a less dangerous playmate than that old moggy,' he said.

A long forefinger traced the barely discernible scar tissue and brought a tingling shiver to her skin, but she still resisted the temptation to look up at him. 'Poor old Thomas!' she reproached him, the caressing finger giving her voice a light unsteady sound. 'I wish your wildcat hadn't escaped, though, Campbell, I was truly sorry about that. How do you think she's faring now?'

'Rearing her own kittens, very likely,' he guessed carelessly. He still held her hand and his thumb rubbed lightly, caressingly over the faint pink mark on her forearm, bringing a fluttering response from her pulse. 'Are you certain you haven't been worse hurt than you're telling me?' he insisted after a moment or two. 'You still look too pale for my liking.'

'No, I'm fine—honestly, Cam.'

'Campbell, damn you.' He reproached her mildly, despite the curse, and she laughed.

'Sorry!'

A swift upward glance caught a look in his eyes that made her heart lurch suddenly as if it had received a shock. 'You will be if you're not very careful,' he warned, and gave her a nudge with his hip as he sat down on the same bale of hay. He must surely know how he could affect her, Chiara thought wildly, and found herself thinking longingly of the times when he would have kissed her in a situation like this. 'Who was driving the other car, Chiara? Anyone we know?'

She snatched her mind back to practicalities again

and recalled the big redhaired man. 'Nobody I knew,' sh
said, 'but Gavin knew him.'

'Oh?'

She mused on the half-remembered features for
moment, trying to keep control of her senses whil
Campbell held her hand in his and pressed it hard in
his strong fingers. 'He was a big man, redhaired an
with blue eyes.' Something struck her then that ha
eluded her at the time, and she looked at Campbell'
craggy profile and red-gold hair. 'I think he might hav
been one of John Roberts' descendants,' she told him
'He's certainly made good, because his suit was well cu
and that car must have cost a fortune, so if he is
descendant——'

'You were very observant in the circumstances,' Camp
bell remarked, then squeezed her hand so hard sud
denly that she protested. 'Hugh Lussie!' he declared. 'I
must have been Hugh Lussie come back!'

'He had a trace of American accent,' she told him, an
frowned curiously. 'Hugh Lussie—wasn't that the nam
you told me——'

'The Lussie boys always have the look of the Robert
on them,' Campbell reminded her. 'He went to Canad
about four years ago.'

Chiara made no effort to disguise her interest. 'Well
he's evidently come back a rich man by the look of him.

Campbell was smiling, a curiously wry smile, and h
shook his head. 'Maybe Betty will be sorry she didn'
marry him after all,' he mused, 'if he's come home
rich man.'

'Betty?' She frowned at him curiously. 'Betty Mc
Donald?'

'The same,' Campbell agreed. 'Hugh Lussie chased he
for years before he eventually gave up and went off t
Canada. He'd have married her too, in spite of every
thing, but he wasn't of a mind to share her, and sh

never seemed to favour him any more than the rest.'

Chiara tugged a length of hay from the bale she was sitting on and nibbled the end of it thoughtfully. 'Maybe because, according to Gavin, she always had a fancy for you,' she suggested, and looked up quickly when he laughed.

'Aye, well,' he said with a sardonic smile, 'it's been proved that the poor lassie is soft in the head, hasn't it?'

'Not any more, apparently,' Chiara told him, refusing to rise to the bait. 'I heard from the Houstons that she's completely better and she's coming home soon.'

'I'm glad to hear it,' said Campbell, and his expression was serious. 'I wonder if Hugh Lussie got wind of that, for she'll surely have more time for him now.'

To Chiara the kind of outlook he attributed to Betty McDonald was inconceivable and she frowned at him doubtfully. 'She surely wouldn't change her mind about him simply because he's come home rich, would she?' she asked, and Campbell laughed shortly and squeezed her fingers.

'I'm sure she would,' he told her softly. 'Not all females have your romantic view of marriage, you know.'

She coloured warmly, reminded of his own mercenary plans, and wished she wasn't so touchy about the subject. At least if he marries her it will give little Robert a father,' she ventured, and Campbell nodded soberly.

'And this time there's a pretty good chance she'll get the right man.'

It was nearly two weeks later when Chiara saw Gavin again, and she had by then taken it for granted that whatever tenuous relationship had existed between them was finished. It did not trouble her unduly, but she had the kind of nature that disliked being at odds with anyone, and she would rather they had parted without that

determined air of self-pity that Gavin had reproached he
with.

It was completely unexpected, and unwelcome, when
he spotted her by the loch one morning and came across
the burn to join her as he had done on an earlier
occasion. But he was cautious, wary even, and he did
not immediately get out of the jeep, but sat for a
moment or two looking at her in silence; and speculating
she thought.

'How are you, Chiara?'

He got out of the jeep as he asked, and she noticed
how often he brushed his hands down the tweed trouser
he was wearing, a gesture that suggested how nervous he
was. 'I'm perfectly O.K. now, Gavin, thank you.' She
didn't want to get involved with him again, but she was
obliged to ask about his sister. 'I understand that Betty
is home again; is she quite better?'

'Aye, she is—thank you.' It was appalling to just
stand there, but they had so very little in common, she
realised. Obviously he had something on his mind and
that did something to arouse her sympathy without her
being quite sure why. 'She—she's to be married, Chiara.'

So Campbell had been right! No matter how hard she
tried it was impossible to keep the harshness out of her
voice. 'To Hugh Lussie?' she guessed, and his look was
enough to confirm it.

'I would guess that Campbell Roberts suggested that,'
he said, and for once his pedantic way of giving Campbell his full name irritated her.

'He thought it was a possibility,' she conceded.

Gavin took off his hat and scratched his thumb back
and forth on his sandy crown for a second, obviously
finding it hard to go on. 'She is—different, Chiara, and
more—honest.' He knew he had her interest at that
point and Chiara waited with a slightly more urgent beat
in her heart. 'Robert is Hugh Lussie's, he willingly ac

cepts the fact, and he is angry that she would have credited another man with his son. He loves her,' he added, as if that was the hardest thing of all to understand. 'He was always wanting to marry her and now that she is over—now that she realises the way things are, she will marry him.'

'And be happy, I hope,' Chiara added from her own generous heart.

There was a bitter irony, she thought, in the fact that Betty McDonald, who would readily have married for gain, was being married for love, while Chiara herself, ready to marry purely and simply for love, had received two proposals both of which were prompted purely by acquisitiveness. It was Gavin's sudden restless shifting of his feet that snatched her back from her moment of self-pity, and she wished it was as easy to dismiss Campbell from her life, as she meant to Gavin McDonald.

'Will you—will you be telling Campbell Roberts how sorry I am?' he asked, and sombre hazel eyes pleaded with her to understand. 'I would tell him myself, but I am not good at explaining, and from you——'

'From me it won't sound the same, Gavin,' she told him, firm even though she sympathised to some extent. It might suggest that I've—arranged it with you; that we have some kind of understanding.'

'And we have not?' he suggested, soft-voiced. She shook her head very definitely and Gavin sighed at the inevitability of it. 'I'm sorry, Chiara, for you are truly the first woman I have ever felt so deeply for.'

'*I'm* sorry,' Chiara told him truthfully, and moistened her lips with the tip of her tongue as she sought for the words she needed. 'I—I think this should be the last time we talk like this, Gavin; I think we should—finish, whatever we had, here and now.'

He didn't expect that, she realised, he didn't expect her to make such a swift, complete break, and for a moment he stared at her unblinkingly with his sharp hazel eyes. Then he turned quickly and without a word and climbed back into the jeep, starting the engine with jerky, stiffly controlled movements. The vehicle shot forward, turned with wheels spinning, then went bouncing and bumping across the heather towards the burn, and as she watched it go Chiara felt a certain regret. But she felt relief as well and she sighed as she turned to make her own way back to Castle Eyrie.

So engrossed was she in thinking about Gavin's sudden and angry departure that she was unaware of anything until Campbell's favourite stallion came up alongside her and made her side-step hastily. Campbell must have seen Gavin driving back across the boundary and she was half expecting some acid remark about his hasty retreat; instead he got down from his horse and started to walk along with her—saying nothing at first, although she could sense that he was watching her.

Long gentle fingers sought and found hers and squeezed her hand lightly. 'Trouble?' he asked quietly and Chiara shook her head.

'No, no trouble.'

'Then what has he done to upset you?'

The probe was gentle but insistent, and she saw no reason to keep it to herself. 'I—I just saw the last of Gavin, I think.'

'And you're sorry?'

There had been a time, Chiara thought, when she would have told him firmly to mind his own business, but she was glad in a way to talk to someone about it. Atagonism from a young man was a new experience to her and she felt oddly chastened by it. 'I'm sorry because it had to end as it did,' she told him. 'He just got into the jeep and—and drove off without a word, and I would rather have parted friends.' She cast him a sideways glance. 'I told him—I suggested that we finished what ever we had between us there and then,' she explained, 'but I didn't mean we couldn't still be civilised to each other.'

'Poor old Gavin!'

He spoke softly and was obviously sincere in his sympathy, so that Chiara, who had been expecting to be the subject of his sympathy, looked at him reproachfully. 'Not poor Chiara, of course,' she said, and he smiled and shook his head.

'You'll never be short of people to love you, Chiara; I think he might.'

Suspecting criticism, however mild, she again glanced at him from the corner of her eye. 'I suppose you think I was too hard on him?' she accused, then hurried on before he could reply. 'I did what I thought was right, Campbell. I don't love him and I'm convinced he doesn't love me, although he's probably—fond of me. I didn't think it was right to go on pretending that there was a chance I might get *more* fond of him, because I know I shan't.'

'You sound pretty sure,' he suggested, and she caught a glimpse of a swiftly arched brow before she went on hurriedly:

'Incidentally, Betty McDonald is getting married to Hugh Lussie, just as you anticipated.'

'Good.' He sounded as if he meant it, and looking at him for a moment, Chiara believed he did. 'He's a good hard worker and Betty's had a hard time of it the past three and a half years; they'll mebbe be good for one another.'

'According to Gavin, little Robert is Hugh Lussie's and he wasn't very pleased about not getting the credit for him; I think it came as rather a shock to Gavin. Having to change his ideas after all this time, I mean,' she explained. 'He's sorry now he accused you.'

'But he wouldn't say so to my face,' Campbell observed dryly, and it seemed automatic to go on as she did, despite what she had said to Gavin when she turned the idea down.

'He *is* sorry, Campbell, he admits it. He—he asked me to tell you so and I said I wouldn't, but—I don't know——'

'You're aye soft-hearted,' Campbell suggested, deep-voiced.

'Maybe.' She had no need to defend herself against such a gentle accusation, she thought. 'I liked Gavin, I still like him, but I don't love him.'

He slipped an arm around her shoulders and hugged her briefly to the once familiar, breathtaking warmth of his body, and his lips just briefly touched her forehead. 'Romantic little nut,' he murmured affectionately, and Chiara's heart fluttered as if he had paid her a compliment. 'By the way,' he went on, 'on a more down-to-earth plane, Alex Murray rang just after you'd gone out——'

'Grandpa's solicitor?'

'That's right. He's coming over tomorrow morning; Grandpa's will has been through probate, or whatever, and we shall know exactly where we stand tomorrow this time.' He studied her for a moment with his disconcerting blue eyes, then heaved a shoulder in a suggestion of shrug. 'I gather we're in for a few surprises.'

'Surprises?' She eyed him curiously, some instinct sending prickles over her scalp. 'What kind of surprises, Campbell?'

'If I knew I'd tell you,' he promised, 'but I don't, so you're as wise as I am until Alex Murray reveals all tomorrow, lass.'

Chiara's heart was hammering hard and fast in her breast and a suspicion lurked at the back of her mind that refused to be banished. She couldn't imagine how it could be true and yet it persisted, and as they walked up the steep incline to the stable yard at the rear of the castle, she voiced it to Campbell.

'I—I have a feeling that Grandpa might have changed his mind,' she ventured above the sound of the stallion's hooves clopping over the cobbles, and Campbell turned his head sharply and looked at her.

'About Castle Eyrie?' he asked, and she nodded. 'Oh no, he wouldn't, Chiara!' He sounded insistent, even slightly indignant, but there was a look in his eyes that suggested nothing would suit him better, and her heart sank. 'Tomorrow will tell,' he said.

CHAPTER NINE

CHIARA still found it hard to believe it had happened, even though she had voiced a suspicion of it to Campbell the day before. Even now that the family solicitor had advised them officially of the contents of a new will, made only two weeks before her grandfather died, she still could not quite believe that he had after all not arranged matters as he had said he wanted them, but left the castle and its estate in its entirety to Campbell. She wasn't angry, since it was what she had expected initially, but she was stunned by the fact of her grandfather having changed his mind so dramatically.

There was a kind of lull for a while after the will was read out and its various legacies explained, and Chiara took advantage of it to try and come to terms with an entirely different situation. She had not been overlooked, in fact under the new will she fared very well, but she had no part of Castle Eyrie itself, and that would require some readjustment on her part.

Campbell and his father were in conversation with the solicitor in the sitting-room, drinking whisky and sharing family news, and Margaret Roberts had disappeared somewhere soon after the bombshell was dropped. Her aunt's feelings were probably rather mixed, Chiara realised, for although she could not pretend to be other than delighted that Campbell was after all sole owner of Castle Eyrie, her relationship with Chiara had altered sufficiently during the past few months for her to appreciate and sympathise with her in her disappointment.

Guessing that she wouldn't be missed, Chiara left the

three men talking and decided to take a walk across the moors. November was a notoriously treacherous month and they had had several days of bad weather lately, but it was dry for the time being and she had an irresistible desire for her own company. The need to think things out was most pressing at the moment, and the cold air would help clear her head as nothing else could.

A thick jacket to keep out the cold, and it would not be too bad underfoot if she stuck to the recognised routes across the moor. She could, she told herself as she set out, easily go back to Italy, for she still had the family house there, unoccupied these past five months or more, but still ready for her whenever she chose to go back there. Although choice, she mused, might not come into it now that her grandfather was gone.

They had been a fairly eventful five months too. Sad and happy, even exciting sometimes, but frustrating too, and in that light she thought particularly of her relationship with Campbell. She could bear to leave Castle Eyrie if she had to, although she had become very attached to it and she would miss its very special kind of atmosphere; she would miss Uncle Colin and even Aunt Margaret now that they were better friends, but mostly she would miss Campbell.

It was the first time she had faced the fact of parting from Campbell, and it startled her to realise just how much she hated the very idea of it. She could actually weep at the thought of leaving, and in fact she brushed a hasty hand across her eyes when she realised there were tears in them. Campbell had what he had wanted all along and he no longer had to consider sharing it with her, so she was no longer necessary to him; he might even be glad to see her go, perhaps allowing for an occasional holiday visit.

It was almost as if thinking about him had conjured up his special pride and joy, for as she brushed the tears from her eyes she noticed the golden eagle go soaring upward into the grey, overcast sky. Old Yellow Nose, Bui Strone; the reason Campbell had driven her out to this same spot what now seemed like a lifetime ago. He had boasted then how fortunate she was to see such a rarity, but she had only since come to understand the reason for his pride.

She followed the bird's flight, fascinated as ever she was, then turned eagerly, catching her breath, when she noticed another and slightly larger eagle lift from the eyrie and take to the air in the harsh east wind, moving with its mate in tight, slow circles above the naked crags. Chiara had never before seen both birds in flight together, and quite instinctively she wished Campbell was there to see it too.

Huge and menacing to those on the ground, but breathtakingly impressive with their great wings, almost seven feet across, spread like dark sails, and their small predatory heads curved downward in a search for prey, they almost hypnotised her. It was so still that the sound of the Land Rover reached her long before it actually got there, and after a brief confirming glance over her shoulder, she returned to her study of the eagles.

Outwardly she appeared unconcerned about the approaching vehicle, but inwardly her whole being was charged with such a chaos of emotions that she felt unable to control them, or even recognise them. She had wished him there and there he was, but not simply to watch the eagles, she knew, and trembled in the knowledge.

She didn't turn even when the Land Rover pulled up several yards from where she stood, and she seemed to feel the ground vibrate with the thud of booted feet coming across the heather towards her. He came to a halt only when he pressed up against her back, and Chiara felt herself arch backwards against him when his warmth flooded through her like wine.

Her gaze did not shift, but her flesh quivered at the touch of the hands that slid beneath her jacket and round her waist, pressing into the yielding softness just below her breasts with long hard fingers. He bent his head and his cheek felt rough on the wind-fresh smoothness of hers, his voice quiet and perhaps not quite steady, very close to her ear. 'I missed you; it gave me quite a bad few minutes when I couldn't find you anywhere. I tried the stable and then I thought I might find you here.'

Chiara half-turned her head, rubbing against the coarser touch of his face, and she put her hands over the ones at her waist, but her eyes were still on the soaring eagles and she indicated them with a very slight movement of her head. 'He has his mate with him today; I've never seen them together before.'

'They're repairing the nest ready for next year's family,' Campbell observed, and the hands at her waist pressed a little harder into her flesh beneath the softness of wool.

Her heart seemed to thud in time with a pulse in his cheek, and Chiara was certain that her legs would never have been capable of supporting her unaided. The long lean length of him curved to accommodate her smaller shape, and his arms felt strong and warm and very much as if they belonged where they were, so that she had a strong sense of contentment suddenly.

'They seem to be circling above the crags,' she pointed out in a voice so breathless it was barely more than a whisper, 'and it's very black overhead. Is it going to storm, do you think?'

'More than likely.'

He still held her close and his eyes still watched the eagles, just as hers did, but she had never studied anything with such apparent interest and so little real attention. The encircling arms and the body that sup-

ported her pulsed with a vigorousness that made her
tremble, and he held her as if he sought to make her part
of his own hard length.

When a large heavy raindrop plopped suddenly on to
her forehead she raised her face to it, closing her eyes
briefly, so that the one that followed it hung and
trembled for a moment on her lashes. Then the drops
became faster and the encircling arms crushed her so
hard for a second that she gasped.

'I'd better take you home,' Campbell murmured, his
voice muffled in her hair, 'before you get another soak-
ing.' He turned his mouth to her cheek and kissed her
with a lingering lightness. 'I've missed kissing you,' he
whispered, and the warmth of his breath mingled on her
cheek with the cooler rain.

She smiled up at him. 'I've missed it too,' she confessed. 'Ever since that day in the stable——'

'Come on!'

He had her by the hand, running before the rapidly increasing rainfall and pulling her along with him. With
a broad grin he almost literally flung her into the Land
Rover, then scrambled in after her, both of them laughing and breathless. Then he leaned across and kissed her
laughing mouth lightly, just before he started the engine
up, and rain rattled and bounced on the bonnet and the
windscreen as they bumped over the overgrown track.
Neither of them said a word, but every so often, as if by
mutual instinct, their heads would turn and their eyes
would meet and smile.

When they drove into the yard at the rear of the castle
it was in a positive deluge, and Chiara was reminded
of another, exactly similar occasion, when Campbell had
come to her rescue in the pouring rain, on horseback on
that occasion. The number of horses they kept had de-
creased a good deal during the past few years, and some
of the stable buildings now served as garage space for
the motor vehicles her grandfather had disliked so much.

Campbell drove in without pause and judged the Land Rover's length exactly so as to miss the end wall. He gave her a swift triumphant smile, then got out quickly and came around to offer her his help, half lifting her from her seat. From the look in his eyes she believed he too remembered that other time, and for that reason if for no other, she flushed and evaded his eyes for a moment.

Still holding her hands, he studied her face, then leaned and kissed her mouth, lightly, almost teasingly. 'O.K.?' he questioned softly, and she nodded without really knowing what he had asked her.

Outside, the cobbles hissed and gleamed in the downpour, rippled and silver grey like running water, and Chiara shook back her hair as they started to run, hand in hand, across the yard. She stumbled and nearly tripped when Campbell veered across to his left suddenly, making for the open door of the stable where the horses were kept instead of the rear door into the castle, taking Chiara with him.

Her heart was beating with a wild, exciting beat that drummed through her head when she remembered trying to get down from the stallion's back without his assistance and knocking them both into the straw, with results that she felt she never could forget. Inside it was shadowed and dim, but dry, and they stood for a second hand in hand and unmoving.

Then the grey stallion shifted in his stall, made restless by the noise of the rain on the roof, and in the vacant stall next door the abandoned wire run that had once housed the wildcat still stood in one corner, its door still swinging open. Chiara was shivering and breathing hard, her cheeks damp and slightly pink, still stinging from the rain, and she looked at Campbell with eyes that had never seemed more huge and black, or glowed more brightly.

His own thick jacket hung open and he began to un-

fasten hers with slow deliberation, holding her slightly
dazed eyes with his own vivid blue ones while he pushed
the collar back from her neck. Sliding his arms around
her, he drew her against him and touched his lips to the
softness of her neck, moving with shivering slowness to
her cheeks and her half-closed eyes, and the cool damp-
ness of her chin and throat, searching, coaxing, seeking
a response until she gave a little moaning sigh and lifted
her mouth to him.

He took it lightly at first, and then with increasing pressure until it was buried deep in the warm urgency of his.
As one, they turned slowly, lips sealed close, and sank
down into the prickly mass of the straw, and it was as
if she had never spoken those reckless, angry words all
that time ago. Just as then, his weight pressed her downward, his hands gentle but demanding, like the mouth
that seemed her only source of life as she clung to it
eagerly.

Then his voice murmured in the muffling tangle of her
hair so that she could scarcely make out the words. 'That
day in the stable?' he prompted, as if she had just that
minute said it.

'You don't know how sorry I was that I—I said what
I did about Betty McDonald,' she murmured, and he
raised his head to look down at her. She had never seen
those blue eyes look as they did then, and raising her
arms she put them around his neck, heedless of the
weight that seemed to be crushing the breath from her
body. 'I missed being kissed by you,' she confessed in a
whisper, and again offered her lips to the hovering, smiling mouth.

'Don't you hate me?' he asked, depriving the word of
its malicious meaning, and Chiara shook her head.

'I never hated you!'

'Not even now you've heard Grandpa's new will?'

'I've never hated you,' Chiara insisted huskily. 'Not
even now.'

For a moment he simply looked at her, then he lightly touched her lips. 'I love you,' he said softly, and Chiara knew he had nothing to gain by saying it now. 'I've loved you for far longer than you realise, my little love.' He kissed her again, then scanned his vivid gaze swiftly over her flushed and smiling face. 'Oh, you've given me some bad moments and you've near sent me crazy with your stubbornness at times, but you've a face on you like a wee black-eyed *bambina*, and I love you!'

Close enough to touch the hard, strong jaw with her lips, Chiara kissed him, but just for a moment her eyes reproached him too. 'Why didn't you tell me you loved me? If I'd known——'

'Away! You'd never have believed me if I had, now would you?'

It was true, Chiara had to admit. Because she had been so sure that he wanted her only as a means of getting his hands on the whole of Castle Eyrie she would never have accepted that he loved her, however much she might have wanted to believe it, and she shook her head. 'No, I suppose I wouldn't have,' she admitted.

'And now?'

Looking up at him, her eyes glowed with a depth of desire she had never even dreamed of until that moment, and she could only wonder how she had managed to resist for so long and so adamantly. 'Now you have nothing to gain by marrying me,' she whispered, 'and I love you so much that I'd marry you even if you had.'

She seemed to have stopped breathing for so long that her head was spinning when he rolled over on to his back and lay there looking up at her with those stunning blue eyes. 'Chiara, Chiara, Chiara.' He repeated her name softly, rolling the 'r' and making it sound as only he could, and she moved closer against him, the upper part of her body resting on him with her hands curved lovingly about his face, her dark eyes glowing between their thick lashes. 'Oh, Chiara! How could I ever have seen you only as a means to an end, my sweetheart?'

She stroked a fingertip across his lips, undeceived even in the excitement of her love. 'But you did!'

'Aye, at first I did.' He had always been brutally honest, she reminded herself, and leaned down to kiss his mouth before she allowed him to go on. 'But then I wanted you more than I ever did Castle Eyrie, and by then you were so suspicious of me that you'd have married Gavin McDonald rather!'

'Oh no, I wouldn't!' Her eyes teased him, for she felt secure in her love. 'At least you were an honest mercenary!'

Sliding a hand beneath her hair, he pulled her down to him and kissed her mouth, a long, lingering kiss, while his fingers twined strongly in her black hair. 'Grandpa knew I'd ruined my chances and he did the only thing he could to help me get you back.'

Her lips parted in surprise, Chiara blinked. 'Do you mean—*that's* why Grandpa made a new will?'

'He knew how desperately I loved you,' Campbell told her softly. 'I think the whole family knew except you, my love, and he knew you'd set your heart against me after that initial gaffe I made. I think he realised that my only chance lay in taking away the cause of your suspicion, but by God, he took a chance! If I'd known what he was up to I'd have tried to talk him out of it; because he wanted you here at Castle Eyrie and you might not have wanted me after all!' She was silent for a moment, her mind busy, and Campbell was eyeing her curiously. 'Chiara? D'you not want me after all, girl?'

'You know I do!' She looked down into his eyes for a moment, but still found it difficult to say what she wanted to say, knowing Campbell and his Roberts pride. 'Campbell—I was wondering. I mean, all the legacies that Grandpa left to various people—there can't be too much left to keep the scheme running, and I have a house, quite a large house in Tuscany——'

'*No*, my love!'

He turned swiftly and she once more found herself pinned down in the prickly cushion of straw by the weight of his body while his eyes gleamed fiercely down at her for a moment. Then they softened and warmed as he looked into her face with its almost childlike look of apprehension. A large hand curved gently about her cheek and he touched her mouth lightly with his.

'No, you keep your house in Tuscany, sweetheart,' he whispered, stroking back her hair. 'Mebbe we'll spend our honeymoon there, but I'll not take it from you. Oh, I'd have taken Castle Eyrie because I felt I had a right to it, but I'll not take your father's house from you.'

'I shall have to sell it——'

'Then buy your trousseau with the proceeds!' Campbell suggested firmly. 'For I'll not touch a penny of it!'

'You're too proud,' she whispered, not seeing it as a fault but as part of his legacy from his grandfather.

'Mebbe,' he conceded, then smiled down at her again. 'We'll cope, lass,' he told her softly, 'you'll see. I have plans, and I'm not the pauper you seem to think me, for I've shares in my Campbell grandfather's distillery too; Father insisted, though I'd no wish for it.'

'And you've got Castle Eyrie.'

'I have you,' Campbell murmured against her lips. 'That's what I need most of all!'

When Chiara was capable of noticing anything as mundane as the weather, she realised that it had almost stopped raining, and somehow resented it because it was like the end of a very special moment. The wet earthy smell of the stable seemed the most romantic scent in the world, and she sighed resignedly when Campbell got to his feet suddenly, then reached down for her hands.

'We'd best let them know we've not been drowned on

the moor,' he said, 'and that there's going to be a wed
ding very soon.'

'Very soon?' Her dark eyes mocked his certainty and
he drew his brows into a menacing frown.

'*Very* soon,' he insisted, and began pulling straws from
her jacket and her tousled hair. Vivid blue eyes glowed
in wicked anticipation of the conjecture their straw-
bedraggled appearance would inspire, and he pulled
her once more into his arms, seeking her mouth with an
abandon that left her breathless. Then with his face
nestled in silky black hair, he smiled. 'At least now I've
no need to ask how to keep the black-eyed brat amused,'
he said.

The Mills & Boon Rose is the Rose of Romance

Every month there are ten new titles to choose from — ten new stories about people falling in love, people you want to read about, people in exciting, far-away places. Choose Mills & Boon. It's your way of relaxing:

April's titles are:

THE STORM EAGLE by *Lucy Gillen*
In other circumstances Chiara would have married Campbell Roberts. But he had not consulted her. And now wild horses wouldn't make her accept him!

SECOND-BEST BRIDE by *Margaret Rome*
Angie would never have guessed how the tragedy that had befallen Terzan Helios would affect her own life . . .

WOLF AT THE DOOR by *Victoria Gordon*
Someone had to win the battle of wills betwwen Kelly Barnes and her boss Grey Scofield, in their Rocky Mountains camp . . .

THE LIGHT WITHIN by *Yvonne Whittal*
Now that Roxy might recover her sight, the misunderstanding between her and Marcus Fleming seemed too great for anything to bridge it . . .

SHADOW DANCE by *Margaret Way*
If only her new job assignment had helped Alix to sort out the troubled situation between herself and her boss Carl Danning!

SO LONG A WINTER by *Jane Donnelly*
'You'll always be too young and I'll always be too old,' Matt Hanlon had told Angela five years ago. Was the situation any different now?

NOT ONCE BUT TWICE by *Betty Neels*
Christina had fallen in love at first sight with Professor Adam ter Brandt. But hadn't she overestimated his interest in her?

MASTER OF SHADOWS by *Susanna Firth*
The drama critic Max Anderson had wrecked Vanessa's acting career with one vicious notice, and then Vanessa became his secretary . . .

THE TRAVELLING KIND by *Janet Dailey*
Charley Collins knew that she must not get emotionally involved with Shad Russell. But that was easier said than done . . .

ZULU MOON by *Gwen Westwood*
In order to recover from a traumatic experience Julie went to Zululand, and once again fell in love with a man who was committed elsewhere . . .

If you have difficulty in obtaining any of these books from your local paperback retailer, write to:

Mills & Boon Reader Service
P.O. Box 236, Thornton Road, Croydon, Surrey, CR9 3RU.

The Mills & Boon Rose is the Rose of Romance

THE McIVOR AFFAIR by *Margaret Way*
How could Marnie kill this feeling of attraction that was growing between her and the hateful Drew McIvor, whom her stepmother had cheated?

ICE IN HIS VEINS by *Carole Mortimer*
Jason Earle was a cold, unfeeling man. Yet, given the right circumstances, Eden could like him altogether too much!

A HAUNTING COMPULSION by *Anne Mather*
Despite the bitterness Rachel Williams felt about Jaime Shard, she accepted to spend Christmas with his parents. But Jaime would be there too . . .

DEVIL'S CAUSEWAY by *Mary Wibberley*
Why did Maria have to complicate the situation by falling in love with Brand Cordell, who was angry and bitter about the whole thing?

AUTUMN IN APRIL by *Essie Summers*
Gaspard MacQueen hoped Rosamond would come and settle in New Zealand, but his grandson Matthieu had *quite* another view of the situation!

THE INTERLOPER by *Robyn Donald*
It was the hard Dane Fowler whom Meredith really feared. All the more so, because of her unwilling love for him . . .

BED OF ROSES by *Anne Weale*
Was her husband Drogo Wolfe's involvement with his 'close friend' Fiona turning Annis's bed of roses into a bed of thorns?

BEYOND THE LAGOON by *Marjorie Lewty*
When her deception was discovered Gideon North's opinion of Susan French would hardly be improved. Why did she care so much?

SUMMER OF THE RAVEN by *Sara Craven*
Rowan was stuck with Carne Maitland, the one man she really wanted — and one who was totally out of reach.

ON THE EDGE OF LOVE by *Sheila Strutt*
Dulcie fell in love with the cold Jay Maitland — only to find that his coldness didn't apply to the beautiful Corinne Patterson.

If you have difficulty in obtaining any of these books from your local paperback retailer, write to:

Mills & Boon Reader Service
P.O. Box 236, Thornton Road, Croydon, Surrey, CR9 3RU.
Available May 1981